Once Upon A

Commune

Abilene Gray

Publisher~Abilene Gray Unlimited

Cover Design by Jamee Farinella
Photographs by Abilene Gray
Author's Photograph by T. D. Leone

For information, please go to: www.abilenegray.com

The cataloging-in-publication data is on file with the Library of Congress.

ISBN 978-0-615-26099-0

December 2009

First Edition

Acknowledgements

To Stephen and Dale, the fathers of my children, who loved me and let me go.

To my children who have no doubt questioned how they got into a family like this one—as Ram Dass[1], my spiritual guide and teacher once said,

"You chose the parents you are born to." You chose us. Really.

"No-o-o-o-o-o!! No-o-o-o-o!!" Catherine wailed at the top of her voice as she stood in the middle of the road facing the farmhouse.

Daniel's car was gone, and she knew, so were her little girls. He had taken them. He had sent her to the store for milk, and he had taken them. When she drove up in front of the farmhouse, she could see the space where his car had been parked. Empty. Gone.

Catherine buckled to her knees in the middle of the road, pounding her fists on the ground while crying, "No! No!" over and over again.

She didn't see, nor hear, her neighbor's approaching truck.

SUMMER 1974

I'm gonna leave this city, got to get away
I'm gonna leave this city, got to get away
All this fussing and fighting, man, you know I sure can't stay
Now baby, pack your leaving trunk, you know we've got to leave today...

Alan Wilson, Canned Heat

"Going Up The Country," *Living the Blues, 1968*

Chapter 1

"All ready, Laura?"

"All ready, Mommy!"

"All ready, Becky?"

"All ready, Mommy!"

"All ready, Daniel?"

"It's going to be a long drive."

It was a bright, warm summer morning in late June. Daniel and Catherine Janson decided to leave Boston early Friday morning to drive to their new summer home in Vermont.

Daniel had checked the small trailer attached to the back of their Volvo station wagon. He could see it in the side mirrors pretty well so he hoped it would be all right.

I sure don't want to have to back up. Maybe we won't need to stop. While mentally checking off the list of things that could go wrong pulling a trailer, he drew his fingers through his thick, brown curly hair. He hadn't had time for a haircut before leaving and now he would have to get one as soon as he returned home. He adjusted the seat again to try to make it accept his height, but that became a fruitless task. Then he touched his new designer sunglasses. He thought about his new case going to trial and looked forward to returning home.

Catherine was excited and could hardly contain herself. But, she had to. She didn't want to aggravate Daniel. He was doing so much to accommodate her these days. First, he agreed to buy a summer home for them to have as a family getaway, and second, gave her the freedom—within reason—to renovate it. She tucked her blonde, shoulder-length hair behind one ear as she turned to check on her daughters. Her fair coloring was in contrast to Daniel's; her blonde hair and eyes of pale, gray-green directly opposed his dark brown hair and distinctive brown eyes.

It seemed to her that their recent arguments had been set aside for this family trip. An unspoken truce had occurred in preparation for their time away.

Catherine looked back at the Boston brownstone they were leaving. *For the summer*, she reminded herself, *just for the summer. If only it could be longer.*

She had had to tell their British nanny, Anna, that they wouldn't need her for two months and would pay for her to "cross the pond"[2] and visit her family while they were at their summer home. She wondered why Daniel thought they needed a nanny at all now that Catherine wasn't going to be working. She hoped he wasn't expecting her to return to those society luncheons with country club women who only talked about their latest shopping trips.

Catherine's background of simpler, middle class roots eschewed the trappings of those her mother termed "show-off moneyed-folk." Her father was a professor at Boston University and her mother was a homemaker. Her two older sisters and three older brothers were not very excited for her when she met and dated Daniel. One family weekend after she and Daniel announced their engagement, her brothers, and their wives, and her sisters, and their husbands, and several nieces and nephews had driven to New Hampshire to pick apples. Daniel couldn't go, of course, as he was just starting out building his own law firm. He rarely went to anything with her family as he preferred the crowd he had grown up with and their social functions. It was familiar to him and comfortable, while her family and friends made him feel like a duck out of water.

Catherine was only too glad to spend the day in doing something she had enjoyed most of her life. Her brothers had literally grilled her about her choice of a future husband, and it lasted most of the day, until her sisters intervened. The incident had saddened her so much that she had never gone apple-picking with her siblings again. After her marriage, her visits to her family grew less and less. Her most treasured memories of childhood were with her whole family going to watch the maple sugaring process in the early spring, picking wild blueberries near a lake they used to go to in the summer, and then apple-picking in the fall interspersed with hikes into the White Mountains. A summer home in the country meant that she could introduce her children to the things she loved of her earlier years—swimming in lakes, hiking in the mountains, and maybe, one day, apple-picking.

Daniel worked hard to make his life the envy of many. He had risen as one of Boston's stellar attorneys, winning the toughest cases, and making more money than Catherine could conceptualize. He had a lot to live up to as his family was a mix of attorneys, judges and a cousin who was a senator. His mother was an attorney at a time when women attorneys were few and far between. And, his father had recently been named a judge. There was no doubt that he and his two sisters would follow suit. And, there were two options after college: Yale Law School or Harvard Law School. Oh, they were encouraged to choose any college they desired, as long as it was Ivy League. Nothing less. As the oldest, he could still remember breaking out in a sweat as he stood in front of his parents and they opened his letters from his applications to law school. Fortunately, he had been accepted to both. He chose Harvard for the proximity of where he would eventually begin his law practice—and he already had many connections from his undergraduate days. He felt tethered to his family and would never leave the Boston area. In time, his sisters followed in his footsteps, became attorneys, but moved as far away as possible—or so his mother said. They gathered for holidays but that was about it. Daniel knew that if he were stronger, and less interested in pleasing his parents, he would have moved far away as well. But, then he wouldn't have met Catherine, someone he felt sure would be the right kind of wife for him and his career. She was unpretentious and lacked the deviousness he had found in his parents' friends' daughters at their prestigious country club. When they met, she was fresh out of college, starting a career in interior design with the best architect and design firm in Boston run by Albert Greenshaw. She had come along to the first meeting as Albert's design associate— she was talented and had been hired by someone who knew.

After their first meeting, Daniel was smitten. An unassuming blonde with smooth, shiny hair and those pale, gray-green eyes, she was at least a foot shorter than he was. He felt protective toward her as she set about doing her job, offering to move things out of her way. She measured his offices and asked questions about his style and his wishes for the project. She brought Albert's drawings to show him, and, in time, some of her additions were also included—partly at Daniel's request. While he was thirteen years older with an established reputation, he compared starting his own law firm with Catherine beginning her career. He tried to show her their similarities, to get her to be interested in him. She seemed shy at first, and then began to recognize that he was interested in her more than for her work.

At the close of her very first project, he took her to dinner and began to court her in a proper manner—something he never had had to do before. She had never asked him how much he earned, what his assets were, or any of the questions other young women had asked him after they dated more than a couple of months. And, she never did.

After they were married, within nine months, Laura was born. Daniel thought Catherine should stay home. Reluctantly, she gave up her budding career and tried to abide by his wishes. Daniel had been the one to interview and hire Anna, because he knew best. He said that Anna had "the correct education and background to take care of Laura" so that Catherine could go to his mother's luncheons and attend the charitable events that had been a constant in his life. At first, it was all quite glamorous and she had been taken shopping by one of Daniel's assistants to get her clothing up to speed. She had her hair done at least every week and certainly before any event.

When Rebecca was born three years later, Catherine was glad she had Anna's assistance, but she began to stay away from some of the events that she used to attend. None of the women she met were friendly and several made comments about her husband which she thought were inappropriate. She knew he had had a life before she came along—but she really didn't need the details. Just because she was younger didn't mean she was completely innocent. Daniel was frustrated with her for dropping out of the public eye and his mother was constantly trying to get her to go to various luncheons by offering to take her shopping. None of it was working.

She had wanted to return to her career after Becky was born—but that became a lot more difficult than she thought it would be.

The end of June in their Boston brownstone had brought a flurry of activity to the Janson household. Since the girls were both born in June, Catherine sold them the idea of celebrating their birthdays together.

"Let's have one party before we leave for the summer! Won't that be fun?" Besides, she reasoned, Laura had already had a school party.

Laura turned six, and she wasn't convinced this was all that great. Becky would turn three, and she would do anything that involved her older sister.

Catherine packed up summer clothes and some warmer jackets for the cool nights they expected to have during their first summer in Vermont.

As the realtor said when they first found the picturesque, immaculately-kept property, it was a "gentlemen's farm," meaning it was not used by those who worked at farming anymore.

The acres of rolling meadow land that surrounded the house and barn had been untouched for about a century. The updates that were already completed included one full bathroom upstairs and one half bathroom downstairs. A connecting shed joined the house to the barn but was unfinished and looked more like part of the barn. It even had a built-in, three-hole outhouse at the back corner so that you could clean it out underneath. Long ago the three-holes had been thoroughly cleaned and boxed in, just leaving the space as a nod to simpler—and less convenient—times. The family that presently owned it liked to stay there for the summer only, and there was no insulation in the house—save some old newspapers and corn cobs. That was the first thing Catherine decided to remedy. Summer evenings in Vermont could be quite cool.

The transforming of the connecting shed between house and barn into a family room wasn't far behind.

Her recent fiasco of attempting to return to work still stung. Albert Greenshaw had been thrilled when she asked to come back, only to have her attempt sputter and fail. She felt torn by the constant interruptions from Daniel, his mother and Anna. It seemed as if they were conspiring against her. Each time she picked up her phone, Albert would roll his eyes.

After their second daughter was born, she thought she could return to work—after all, she had a full-time nanny. Her obstetrician-gynecologist, who had delivered her two children, had come down on her with such wrath during their conversation at her six-week check up that she could still recall the sound of his voice.

"So, Catherine, how's everything going?" Dr. Charles Cohen said.

"Fine," Catherine replied, "I've been thinking about returning to my old job."

"What? You have a newborn! What is wrong with you? Does your husband know?" said Dr. Cohen.

"I'm going to tell him when his present trial is over. He's been really busy—"

"He's a trial lawyer! What are you going to do with two children when he has to work late and needs to come home to rest?"

"Well, I have our nanny, Anna and I could get a babysitter if—"

"If I were your husband, I'd slap you!" Dr. Cohen interrupted.

Catherine had left the appointment feeling ashamed and humiliated. She waited two more weeks to bring it up to Daniel, no longer feeling so confident. Some of her friends had to work to help out—she didn't have to work and she wanted to. She knew Daniel would have plenty to say as well.

"It'll never work," Daniel had said. "They are too little and you can't count on everything working out as planned."

After a few months of attempting to work at her former design firm, with missed deadlines and the need to cancel meetings when one of her daughter's was sick, she gave her notice and gave up the struggle. She was thankful that Daniel hadn't repeated his admonition—"It'll never work." It hadn't. He was right. Catherine felt defeated. Even Albert thought it was for the best.

Trying to balance working, caring for her children and being a good wife to her husband, the juggling act and endless frustrations exhausted her. All the help from Anna didn't seem to make the difference she thought it would. Daniel and his mother called her several times a day while she was working with important discussions that couldn't wait. After she left the interior design firm and the work that she loved, although saddened by her failure, she thought it would perhaps make her marriage better.

The chance to turn the connecting shed into a family room at the farmhouse had been a form of compensation by Daniel for Catherine giving up her career. He always told her just to wait awhile until they went away to school.

"Just a few more years, Catherine," he had said.

Catherine didn't want her daughters to go away to school. College was soon enough.

Daniel's mother recognized that Catherine was feeling low from her work fiasco and had recommended her own, personal psychiatrist, Dr. Bernstein.

When she mentioned to Dr. Bernstein that her ob-gyn doctor thought she should be institutionalized for wanting to have a career just because she was a wife and mother, Catherine expected Dr. Bernstein to protest.

Instead, he said, "Might be a good idea for an evaluation, Catherine. You know, rule out anything serious."

She continued to see him, thinking she could prove that there was no reason for her to be 'evaluated.'

Daniel agreed to let her oversee the family room project including a fireplace, closets and shelving, updating the loft—like she would have done in her job. And, to let her decorate the interior and add furnishings that she wanted. Catherine had spent the past month on the phone with the owner of a small, local business, Richardson's Carpentry, who were used to updating old farmhouses for the city folk. She had heard the term, "flatlanders" more than once. She got it. She understood the point. But, regardless of how modern Jack Richardson's carpenters were, Catherine was interested in keeping the renovations consistent with the circa 1800 farmhouse—not changing it. The next two months lay ahead of her with limitless possibilities, and challenges—not one of which would be to convince the carpenters to maintain the home's authentic essence.

We finally have a summer home, thought Catherine. She knew she was more excited than Daniel who would have to commute weekends from his law firm in Boston. She had lobbied hard to convince him that this particular country home on an old dirt road, that was miles from the nearest town, was just what they needed as a family. A place where they could go away and leave their hectic, overbooked lives behind. She hoped to find solitude and the refuge she so much desired. The added pleasure of being able to influence the design of the connecting shed, and decorate the interior, was frosting on her cake.

Catherine turned to the back seat to encourage the girls to sing as they enjoyed it so much on long car trips. One of their newest learned songs, "Green Grow the Rushes, O,"[3] was fairly long and had many verses to remember.

Laura turned her head side to side, her long, blonde pigtails swinging back and forth. While Laura knew more of the actual words, Becky made up for it with her happy mispronunciations and humming. Becky's brown pigtails bobbed too and fro while she tried to mimic her older sister.

Daniel let out a small groan, and then smiled a little. "Really? You're all going to sing all the way to Vermont? It's at least two and a half hours."

Laura and Becky kept singing while Catherine smiled at Daniel, keeping her hand moving back and forth in the song's rhythm for the girls to follow. "Just a little bit to get the trip going. It's so much fun for the girls to sing. Anna thinks it's wonderful that they can learn so many songs."

Daniel checked in the rearview mirror for the attached wagon that carried some furnishings and extra pieces they didn't need in their town home.

Becky's brown, curly hair matched Daniel's while Laura's blonde, straight hair was closer to Catherine's. But, both girls resembled their dad. He was tall and long-limbed, carrying himself in great strides which caused Catherine to rush to keep up. She knew her girls, who were born with long legs, would one day be tall like their dad. At 6'4", he towered over her and she thought her daughters probably would too. His ruddy complexion could not be confused with most city-pale skin, and he always looked very put together. Even now, in a pair of Levi's, his shirt was neatly tucked in and his belt matched his casual loafers. Catherine and the girls had dressed in pink matching t-shirts and OshKosh B'Gosh overalls. She already had a spot of coffee on her overall strap.

Several songs later, and a sleepy silence overcame them as the rhythm of the highway droned on. Catherine felt herself nodding off and checked the backseat. Both girls were asleep, Laura leaning to one side, Becky's head back with her mouth open. They were so excited they couldn't sleep last night, Catherine recalled, *they must be exhausted.*

"Are you okay, Daniel?"

"Yup. Fine."

Catherine leaned her face toward her passenger window and began to drift off, remembering when they found the farmhouse last fall and she had dreamt about it, over and over.

At the time, they had explored several possibilities for a summer home. But, when they drove up the country road, she fell in love with the entire setting of the old house surrounded by ancient pines shaped like giant Christmas trees and large, gnarled maples lining the road. A blanket of maple leaves covered the road and yard which made everything look untouched, like a photograph on a postcard.

Finally, when Daniel had bid on the property last winter, it was theirs. On a wintry March day, when she attended the closing with Daniel and their attorney, Jake Moll, she couldn't wait to drive up the road again, walk through the house again, and examine every nook and cranny.

After the closing, they took Jake to lunch at Bell's Inn where they were staying. Jake commented on how surprised he was that they bought a summer home so far from Boston, instead of on the Cape, or North Shore, like everyone else in their social set.

"Jake, after lunch would you like to go to the farmhouse and see it? It's really quite wonderful!" exclaimed Catherine.

"Thanks, Catherine, it's so cold here and there's still so much snow. I think I better head back to Boston in case another storm comes in. I would not want to be stuck here!"

As soon as lunch was over, he made a beeline for the snowy, rutted parking lot, leaving them trailing behind trying to wave good-bye.

When they walked back inside the inn, Catherine was shivering. The innkeeper, Mr. Bell, asked, "Are you staying for the town meeting?"

"When is the town meeting?" asked Catherine.

"First Tuesday every March—so it's this coming Tuesday."

"Oh, Daniel, let's stay for the town meeting.[4] Please? I would really love to go to it." Catherine clasped her hands in front of her chest and looked up at Daniel.

Mr. Bell continued, "Mrs. Dingy up the road will have her pies for sale, and they are pretty darn good, if I do say so. They always serve coffee and sweet buns—you don't want to miss that, and my wife makes the best cinnamon buns you ever tasted. And, I hear they are votin' on whether or not to have a kindergarten this year. That'll raise taxes if they do, doncha know."

"Oh, please, Daniel, let's stay! Just one extra night! We can go home right after the meeting!"

Daniel felt exasperated and annoyed, but he was under scrutiny now from the innkeeper, and several other people in the Inn's café who were watching the whole scenario.

"Well, I will have to check with my parents about keeping the girls another night—"

"Oh, thank you! Let me get another sweater upstairs and then we'll go over to the house for a walk through."

Before Daniel could even turn around, Catherine ran up the staircase, leaving him looking at the stairs.

"You wanna use the phone here at the desk?" asked Mr. Bell.

"No, no thank you." Daniel turned toward the door and went outside to call his parents on the pay phone. And, it wasn't one more night—it was two more nights. He had planned to head back on Sunday. He would have to call his office and make sure his calendar was clear on Monday, as it usually was, so that he could prepare for the week. Also, maybe he had a couple of meetings Tuesday that would have to be rescheduled, even if it didn't take all day to go to a little Vermont Town Meeting.

Leaving the girls in Boston with Daniel's parents was his idea, thinking it would take less time for them to assess what was needed in the farmhouse prior to staying there for summer vacation. He thought they would be able to get through the details quickly without having to stop and start for his daughters' needs and could leave first thing Sunday morning. He felt like Catherine had blindsided him again. First, the summer home in Vermont surrounded by mountains—instead of a perfectly good Cape Cod vacation home right near the ocean. Her reasoning was that she would be the one there most of the time, and Vermont was the place she liked the best. Now, they would have to suffer the extra days in this wintry tundra to be involved in some small town politics in which Daniel had no interest.

Staying at the local inn had further unimpressed him. He didn't like the homey, comfortable rooms with quilts, and was shocked that the bathroom was across the hall. There were no telephones or televisions in the rooms. There was one TV in the downstairs living room where everyone could gather in the evening. *Like that's going to happen*, he thought.

Catherine loved everything. Every bit of difference from her daily city life pleased her to no end. Daniel, normally the outgoing, loquacious one had become much more reserved, and Catherine became the friendlier, more interested one in their new Vermont beginnings. Where Daniel was dipping in a toe, Catherine was jumping in head first, curious and interested in every new thing she came across. While no snowstorms were forecast, it was still like winter with snow-covered roads embraced by high, white embankments. They really noticed it driving up to the farmhouse when the station wagon slid a little on the hard-packed finish.

Catherine pointed out how white the snow was, even on the roads, in comparison to the gray slush on the city streets and sidewalks. Finally, Tuesday came and she enjoyed entering the historic town hall building where the Annual Town Meeting was held, looking at the structure and details with eyes wide open.

"What a lovely building!"

"Uh-huh."

They took their place at the end of the line. As they reached the front of the line, a woman sitting at a table handed them a lined sheet of paper on a clipboard. As she glanced up at them above her eyeglasses, she asked, "Are you new-comers?"

Catherine blinked. "Well, yes, I guess we are—we just bought the Sheldon place!"

"I'm Susie Brown. Property owners need to sign the sheet. Shame about it not being farmed anymore. Damn shame. Have you thought about what you're going to do with all that land?"

"Why, no—"

"Well, my husband, Jimmy will cut your fields for the hay if you'll just let it grow. We keep 50 head-a cow and can use all the hay we can get."

Catherine said, without checking with Daniel, "Of course, sounds like a perfect idea!" When she had turned to Daniel, he had just nodded. He thought he would address this later as he scrawled his signature on the list.

They were funneled toward rows of folding chairs, lined up for the Town Meeting. She was glad she hadn't worn her fox fur coat. As it was, she felt overdressed in her casual clothes as everyone seemed to be in flannel shirts and work boots with great, quilted jackets. Daniel's classic camel hair coat stood out like a sore thumb, but they would leave for Boston afterward and he had to go directly to his office. They moved along the line to the table where a coffee urn and cinnamon buns were laid out. They got coffee in a Styrofoam cup and sat down near the back. Catherine was fascinated by the process. She could tell by the way Daniel was looking around that he couldn't wait for a chance to leave.

When the meeting was called to order, a list of issues was presented to be addressed, most of which Catherine didn't know anything about. She listened attentively and hoped to pick up some clues as what they were discussing that was important to the townspeople. Daniel was fidgeting with his hands folding and unfolding them in his lap, looking down and then around the room moving his head carefully so as not to look too curious.

When the kindergarten discussion began, one of the town's elders stood up to speak against it. He was a big, bear of a man and had a florid complexion and a misshapen nose as red as his red suspenders.

"Kindergarten is just babysittin' kids when they could be helping out on the farm or learnin' to do things at home."

Catherine's mouth nearly dropped open. It was like something out of an old—and very bad—movie.

Catherine and Daniel exchanged glances. When it came time to vote, Daniel nudged her arm and they had quietly snuck out.

Drowsily, Catherine opened her eyes to realize she was shivering in the air-conditioned station wagon. As she returned from the wintry memory, she glanced to the lush, green sides of the highway. It was a hot, summer's day outside.

At last, the long, dirt road opened up before them with leafy maples creating an arbor overhead.

"Isn't this road beautiful, Daniel?"

Daniel looked toward the rear of the station wagon where the trailer was moving back and forth.

"I'll feel better when I can get this trailer off the car."

Catherine looked back, but only as far as her two daughters' sleeping faces. When they had both drifted off, she knew as soon as the car stopped, they would probably wake up.

The engine strained as it climbed the last hill, past the ancient cemetery.

There, on her left, stood the barn in all of its pristine glory. Catherine loved the barn, as it was clean as could be, and smelled only of a distant memory of hay. Then, the connecting shed to the house that would become their new family room appeared. It had a door like the front of the house, and she thought it would make a nice entry area instead of the front door. She envisioned a place for jackets, boots and shoes.

And finally, the perfect, quintessential farmhouse against the backdrop of the surrounding hills. As it looked down over the landscape offering bucolic views of the green meadows, it seemed to be welcoming them; all dressed up with a freshly cut front lawn and shiny, clean windows. Catherine breathed a sigh of contentment as Daniel navigated the station wagon and trailer off the road in the space in front of the connecting shed. She opened the door as the car came to a stop and jumped out, running across the path and up the steps to the front porch. She couldn't wait to open up the house before bringing in everything from the car and trailer.

"Hey, Catherine, I'd like a hand here!"

"Be right back!"

Catherine fumbled with the keys and the door popped open before they were fit into the lock.

"Daniel, the door isn't locked."

"Oh, I forgot to tell you. That guy, Jack something, who has been working on the insulation said that he would unlock it this morning. The lock works really hard and will probably have to be replaced."

She entered the front hallway, facing the narrow stairs, and crossed into the parlor. She went right to the windows and opened them up to let in the fresh air. She moved through the downstairs opening a window in every room.

"Catherine, come on, will you?"

As she opened the kitchen windows in the back of the house, she heard Daniel's voice and darted out through the parlor and the front door.

"Sorry, it just smells a little musty so I opened up all the windows."

Daniel was dragging a piece of furniture off the back of the trailer while the girls slept on.

Catherine helped him unload the pieces, the trunks of clothing and the toy boxes—one for each girl. Then, the boxes of books that she had to bring for the summer were all that were left. They took turns carrying each end of each trunk and wrestled them to the porch. As they began unloading the rest of the odds and ends, Laura and Becky woke up.

Catherine opened the car door, Laura bounced out, but Becky was rubbing her eyes. "You want to come out, honey?"

"Okay, Momma."

"Can I go in the house?" asked Laura.

"Of course! Daddy and I put your toy boxes in the front parlor. Go see!"

She reached over to Becky and pulled her toward her, lifting her up and carrying her into the house. "Aren't you a sleepy girl?"

Becky blinked and looked around. She rubbed her eye with a little round fist as they went up the stairs and into the front hallway.

"It smells funny."

"Soon, it will smell like fresh, clean, Vermont air!" exclaimed Catherine, as she walked into the parlor and set Becky down on a rocking chair that they had kept from the few furnishings that were left. A pair of rocking chairs, an ottoman, an uneven table and a shotgun mounted over the fireplace mantel filled out the parlor. The dining room contained an ancient, wide board for a table, which she thought looked just right. And, there were quite a few chairs to seat about a dozen people. A built in corner cupboard held open shelves for dishes. A second parlor could be turned into Daniel's study so he would have a place to work when he was there on weekends. There were a couple of chairs and a table to use for now. The bedrooms upstairs all had bureaus that would work until the new furniture arrived. The old beds were full-sized and their chosen bedroom had had to be cleared out to make space for a king-size bed.

It took the rest of the day to figure out where things would go since there weren't many closets for storage and the house was broken up into four rooms on each floor. Under the front staircase a small, tilted closet was housed where they could put their jackets if they hung them tight to the top. And, for the time being, they could put rain boots and the girls' riding boots inside the small space as well, but Catherine already pictured more closet storage in the not-yet-created family room. The back staircase led to the hall that connected the kitchen and the shed to the barn. No closet space there.

She checked downstairs to see if there was any place to store anything in the basement. The basement had a packed dirt floor which was typical for the time. The posts that held up the ceiling and floor overhead were made of wood. And, it was damp. *No place there to store or leave anything that could grow mold,* she thought.

They went upstairs to complete the sleeping arrangements and get the beds ready for their first night. When the Richardson's Carpentry people had begun working on insulating the house, Catherine had arranged for new full-sized mattresses to be delivered for three of the four bedrooms. The king-size bed had arrived with a separate base. She was glad that that was taken care of as some of the old mattresses showed tears and ripped fabric—probably from mice. She wondered how they would keep mice out of such an old house with so many possible ways to enter. The fireplaces were closed up but the center chimney had a small door where you could look down into the basement and up to the second floor.

The girls helped Catherine make up all the beds with new sheets of beautiful floral prints from Newbury Street specialty shops. The blankets were silky cashmere and cotton blends because of Catherine's sensitivity to wool.

The girls had their own bedrooms for the first time. They had always shared a bedroom in the city and she wasn't sure Rebecca would be ready to sleep in her own room, but Laura really wanted to give it a try. She would start first grade in the fall and she was looking forward to going to school.

The back bedroom would be Daniel and Catherine's. She took care not to put extra pillows on the bed and to keep it streamlined the way Daniel liked it. But, the front bedroom, or guest bedroom, she could design it just the way she wanted it to be. She could hardly wait to get started.

The picnic sandwiches she had brought in the cooler would have to do for lunch. They had thermoses of water, apple juice, and a bag of apples and oranges. By mid-afternoon, their energy had waned.

"Let's go to town and get an early dinner at that little restaurant we went to when we came up here last spring," suggested Daniel.

"Sure, that's a great idea," said Catherine. "Afterwards, if the market is open, we can pick up some groceries. I need to fill the refrigerator."

"Good, let's do it."

While placing fresh towels in the upstairs full bathroom, Catherine called the girls.

"Come and wash up, girls, we're going to town for dinner!"

No response. She could hear small voices off the hall.

She poked her head into Laura's bedroom. They were sitting side-by-side on the bed and Laura was reading *Little House on the Prairie* to Becky.

"Momma, the girl in this book has the same name as me!"

"Yes, she does, doesn't she?"

"But the younger sister is named Mary."

Becky asked, "Can I change my name to Mary?"

"Of course." Catherine smiled.

Daniel unhitched the trailer from the station wagon, and they once again loaded themselves into the Volvo for the trip to town. He couldn't help but think about the many dirt roads that left dust streams behind them. He had grown up in Cambridge and now lived in Boston. Spending time in the country wasn't part of his education. He felt relieved when they finally got onto the paved roads.

A good ten miles and about twenty-five minutes later, and they were on the main street of the small town with Whitey's Restaurant right in the middle. Daniel pulled into the driveway that wrapped around to the back and parked the car.

It was only 5:30 p.m. and the place was packed. If they were going out to dinner in Boston at one of their favorite small places with the girls, it would have been empty at that time.

A booth opened up and soon they were seated. Their waitress welcomed them and said her name was Pam as she pointed to the name tag on her lapel.

"Have you just moved to town?" Pam asked.

"No, not really," responded Daniel, "we're just those 'flatlander' summer people."

"Oh, ha ha," said Pam. "Well, I hope you enjoy your summer." She smiled and winked at Catherine as she handed them menus.

After she walked away, Catherine asked, "Is that necessary?"

Daniel grinned. "Beat 'em at their own game. What do you think they call us?"

Later, Catherine asked Pam if she lived nearby only to learn she had grown up there, and so had her husband. He was the cook at the restaurant. Catherine was intrigued, and later asked Daniel if she could invite them over, but he wasn't interested in getting to know them socially.

"She's a waitress, and her husband is a cook, not a chef."

"So what? That has nothing to do with anything. Besides, they live here, and they will know about the town and the area."

"Naww, let's not. I don't want the local people getting to know my business."

It was their first night in the farmhouse and Catherine slept fitfully, dreaming of pieces of the past spring when things had gotten more and more difficult between her and

Daniel. Then, she heard a flapping sound and sat bolt upright in bed.

"Daniel! Do you hear that? Daniel! Wake up!"

"What—what is it?"

"Something is in the house!"

Daniel was exhausted from the day, but struggled to sit up and turn on the light. At that moment, a bat swooped into their bedroom with about a twelve-inch wingspan.

"Ahhhhhhh!!!" Catherine shrieked. "AHHHH!"

"Stop, you'll wake the girls!" But Daniel didn't move.

The bat sailed back out of the room, careening into the bathroom.

Catherine jumped out of bed just as Laura woke up.

"Mommy? What's going on?" called Laura.

"Stay in your room, honey. It's a bat." Catherine crossed the hall quickly, peeked in to reassure her and closed the door. She shut the bathroom door, hoping the bat was still there. Then checked Becky who was sleeping soundly. When she turned around, she walked into Daniel who had been right behind her.

"Oh! I thought you were still sitting on the bed!"

"No, I got up, too," he said, sheepishly.

"Let's open Laura's door and let her know it's all right."

They walked into Laura's room who was sitting up, wide awake.

"Do you want something to drink, honey?" asked Catherine.

"No, but I have to go to the bathroom."

"That's okay. Let's go downstairs and use that one."

"Okay." Laura took Catherine's hand as she walked out of the bedroom.

When they walked down the back stairs, she realized the house had moths flying about the night light in the kitchen. The telltale buzz of mosquitoes was in the background. When they turned on the bathroom light, Laura had some red marks on her arms. Catherine looked at her own arms, and saw red bug bites as well. She looked at the open window. "Of course, no screens!"

Daniel and Catherine ran around the house, shutting all the windows. In the morning, Daniel called Richard's Carpentry only to have the telephone ring and ring. He had a bill in his wallet with Jack's name and address. The local phone book in the kitchen drawer had his home number. When he called, Jack wasn't at home, but his wife took the message.

When Jack returned from fishing that morning, his wife, Thelma, greeted him at the door. She was dressed in an old plaid house dress and leather moccasins, her apron covered with flour from baking bread.

"Guess who left their windows open all night and don't have any screens?"

"Ha, ha, really? The Jansons? They must be bitten by mosquitoes pretty bad!" He moved the chewing tobacco to the other side of his mouth and spat outside before following his wife into the kitchen. His blue, cotton t-shirt had tobacco juice stains, and his carpenter pants showed paint marks down the sides and wear at the knees.

"They got a bat," she chuckled.

"Naw, really? Geezus. I bet they want screens like yesterday."

"You know it."

Chuckling, Jack sat down to have a cup of coffee and a slice of fresh homemade bread.

The farmhouse was warm with all the windows closed, but Daniel had peeked into the upstairs bathroom and the bat was gone. They had systematically checked all through the house. There were no blinds to close inside against the hot, summer sun. Jack had called back and said he could probably get screens on the house pretty soon. "I hadn't planned to be there Monday, but I'll come over and measure the windows. My crew starts Monday anyway, so it shouldn't be too much trouble to get it done in a couple of days."

"A couple of days?"

"Ayup. Should be about that. See you Monday." And Jack hung up.

Daniel was surprised Jack didn't want to come over right away. He was used to having things done for his schedule. *Unbelievable, I have to wait for these backward, country bumpkins.*

He had to drive to the next town and return the trailer Saturday afternoon. Daniel thought he could rent a car at the same time only to learn that they were two separate businesses. The car rental place was closed on Saturdays. He needed to return to Boston Sunday, but he didn't want Catherine to be without a car so far from town. The man at the trailer rental counter said there was a bus stop that went to Boston a few towns away.

Catherine wanted him to stay over and offered to drive back to Boston. They could stay over one night and return to Vermont the following day.

"That makes no sense. You are just getting settled in here. I might as well just take the bus, but I need to go on the Sunday bus. If I wait till Monday I will lose half the day."

"But, there are no screens for the windows, and it's hot."

"I know, but the workmen are coming Monday to set up and will need to be able to measure the windows and get into the house. Plus, you don't want them roaming around the house when no one is here. We don't know who they are."

In the end, Catherine agreed with Daniel. It made more sense to stay and have the car.

Catherine, Laura and Becky drove Daniel to the bus station which took almost an hour. He didn't have to carry anything with him except for his small traveling case. He left old clothes and the kinds of things he didn't usually wear in the city.

They waited for the bus to arrive and for Daniel to get on it and wave. Then, Catherine and the girls returned to the farm for a week with just the three of them.

"I wish Daddy didn't have to go," said Laura.

"Me, too," said Becky.

"I know, but he'll be back Friday night."

Catherine wasn't sure how she felt. On one hand, it would be nice for him to be there as they got settled in. On the other, she could get out and about with Laura and Becky and meet new people. She would find the stores they needed and learn more about the area. Maybe even have time to join the local library.

On Sunday, as she drove through town, everything except the restaurant was closed. When they got back to the farmhouse, she wanted to explore the barn since it would be cooler there. As they climbed up the stairs and explored, Catherine noticed a stack of small screens that were piled on an old work table.

"Look! Those are screens! We can put them in the windows and open them all up!"

Laura and Becky helped her carry them back through the shed and into the house.

Laura looked doubtful, scowling like Daniel.

"Gee, Momma, they don't look like screens."

"I know, but when I was a little girl, we had them in New Hampshire at our summer cabin."

They started on the first floor. She showed the girls how they slid apart to fit inside each window. They were only about a foot high, but at least they would have some breezes when the afternoon came and the sun's rays began to cool down.

...We are stardust
We are golden
And we've got to get ourselves
Back to the garden...

Joni Mitchell,

"Woodstock," *Ladies of the Canyon,* 1970

Chapter 2

Jack Richardson arrived at 7:00 a.m. Monday morning, ready to measure the windows for the screens. His crew was already parked and unloading saw horses, tools, and their equipment to carry into the connecting shed. Catherine and the girls were still asleep.

Jack knocked on the front door. "Hullo! Hullo!"

Catherine woke quickly, grabbed a cotton bathrobe from the back of the bathroom door, and ran down the front stairs.

"Didn't wake you up, did I?" asked Jack.

"Yes, you did, but that's okay," said Catherine, smiling.

"I want to get the measuring done so I can go over to the next town where the hardware store carries these odd-sized screens."

As Jack entered into the parlor, he noticed the sliding screens in the windows.

"Hey, do you still want new screens? It looks like you found the screens that go with the house."

"Oh, yes, we still want them. They should probably have storm windows attached as well."

"Sure, I can get those for you, but they will have to be ordered. I just need to measure downstairs and upstairs, then I'll be on my way."

"Go ahead, Jack, I'll put on a pot of coffee."

"Okeydokey."

By the time Jack was finished, the coffee was brewed and Catherine was sitting groggily at the small kitchen table, blowing on her mug to cool it down.

"Your young-uns are sound asleep," he said.

"I'm sure the excitement of the change has tired them out," responded Catherine, as she poured him a mug of steaming coffee.

"They'll like it here; I bet they won't want to go back when summer's over," Jack smiled. "T'won't be the first time that happened!"

"They might not be the only ones," she said, grinning, "I already feel like I have finally come home."

After a friendly, albeit short, conversation, Jack took his leave and headed out to find the screens with storm windows for her. He could have them in place by the end of the week if they were ordered right away.

Most of the rest of the week's time was spent talking with the carpenters who came to set up their large, outside saw in the area where Catherine had been parking the station wagon. She moved it out of the way so that they could enter through the barn and have easy access without coming through the farmhouse.

It seemed every time she was leaving with Laura and Becky to take a walk or a drive to town, there was another question to be answered, and one of the three men would saunter over to her before she could get away.

The first few nights were so quiet, Catherine moved into the guest room in the front of the house. She could hear the inside of the house better, including the downstairs, and even though it seemed safe, it was very strange sleeping in such dense silence. The telephone hadn't rung once since they had arrived. That was heaven.

Her dreams were colorful reviews of the events of the past year where she kept trying to find the path she had taken that led her further away from Daniel. *Had it started*

*when she wanted to return to her job working for Albert?
Had it started when she became involved in the anti-war
demonstrations?* Her best friend, Nina, and she had done
everything together. They had both gotten married near the
same time, had gotten pregnant fairly close together, and
had become more tuned in to the political unrest the
Vietnam War had brought. Nina and her husband, Barry
Stone, attended the same charitable events in formal attire
with all the local glitterati. But, recently, they began to
miss some of them. Catherine asked Nina about it and she
said that she and Barry wanted to do "less opulent"
charitable giving. When Catherine brought it up to Daniel,
he was defensive. He liked things the way they were and it
was good for his law firm to be seen at these events—not to
mention the size of his donations. Catherine had hoped it
would inspire Daniel to look at all these functions
differently, maybe pick a few less to attend.

In the late sixties, Nina and Barry instigated a New
York weekend for them all to see the off-Broadway musical,
Hair, and Nina still teased Catherine about it. Nina was
taller than Catherine and had been letting her blonde hair
grow longer, wearing it in one braid. Barry had dark curly
hair like Daniel, but had let it grow out into an Afro[5]. They
had told Daniel that they were dressing in hippie clothes
for the weekend so she and Daniel went to Lord & Taylor's
to be outfitted in the latest hippie style. Catherine had
gotten a white, sheepskin vest, lavender silk shirt with

matching purple silk pants, and white, patent go-go boots. Daniel had found a soft, leather vest with a puffy-sleeved Tom Jones' shirt[6] and bell bottom pants.

They met Nina and Barry at the airport who were dressed in ripped jeans, faded denim work shirts and military jackets.

Catherine was dismayed. "I thought you said you were going to dress like hippies."

Nina saw her expression and said, "Well, you and Daniel are the upper class ones." Then she and Barry laughed, and Catherine and Daniel laughed, too.

Catherine was so taken by the music, she stood and sang along. Daniel had been mortified. When the cast ran through the audience, choosing people to bring up on the stage, a cast member took her hand. Daniel held her arm and pulled her back into her seat. Nina had found it very amusing, saying, "Don't run off with the circus, little girl!" Then, they all laughed, casting amused looks her way. Catherine had tried to laugh, too.

Soon after that, Catherine read about the *Woodstock Music & Art Fair* in the Real Paper and she wanted to go, but Daniel was absolutely against it. She was furious about not attending the event of her generation. She watched it on television, learning the lyrics to the song Joni Mitchell wrote, "Woodstock."

Daniel said at the time, "See? Even Joni Mitchell didn't get to go. You would have hated being there in the mud and rain. Why do you even think it would have been fun?"

Nina and Barry had left their boy, Erin, with her parents and made the trip to New York. However, when they arrived, they had run out of tickets and let everyone in for free. They had found some people with a little tarp to share and made it through the mud and rain. When they returned, they said it was the best experience of their lives. Catherine felt miserable.

From getting their hair done on Newbury Street, going to the country club with their children, and meeting for dinner at the hottest charity events, the two couples had seemed to be in lockstep. But, Barry espoused many of the counterculture changes that were effectively dividing the generations. Both he and Nina were involved in the antiwar movement. The thing was, Barry worked for his father and his future was assured. Daniel had developed and succeeded at his own law practice, something Catherine felt he was still trying to prove to his mother and father.

Daniel disliked her getting involved in demonstrations while he was expanding his own firm. He catered to old Bostonians and wished to keep a low profile, particularly politically. He often dashed home to have supper with Catherine and their children at 6:00 p.m. before returning to his office. But, her pet peeve was that he also turned on the television, to catch up on the day's news, while they were supposed to be having a meal together. One evening at the dinner table, when Daniel switched on the television, there was Catherine being carried off the State House steps.

The newscaster stated, "More than one thousand demonstrators blocked the steps to the State House today—many locally known anti-Vietnam war activists. There's Catherine Janson, wife of the well-known attorney, Daniel Janson, being carried down the steps now—"

Daniel switched off the television and turned to face her, shouting, "This is why I pay for a nanny to help you? So you can go out in public and demonstrate like some hippie? Are you trying to ruin me?"

"I'm sorry, Daniel. I didn't know there were television crews filming me."

"I've made a successful law firm to provide for you and our children for what—so you can embarrass me in public? Do you know what I will have to put up with for the next month just to calm this down?"

The children began to cry. Catherine mumbled another apology and moved to comfort her daughters. Daniel stormed out of their brownstone, slamming the door so hard that the dishes rattled.

It was later that night when Daniel came home that all of the anger he had been controlling spilled out.

"I've put up with a lot, lately, Catherine—Catherine, are you awake?"

"I'm awake."

"You need to know that this is my town. That my family's influence and reputation is important here."

Silence.

"Catherine?"

"What?"

"Are you listening to me?"

"Maybe we shouldn't be together, Daniel..."

"What? What did you say? Don't even think about it! If you try to divorce me, I'll put you in an institution so fast your head will spin! You'll never see our daughters again! Have you got that?"

Catherine froze still, her head on her pillow, eyes wide open.

"Have you got that, Catherine?"

"Y-yes, yes," her voice quivering. All night, she lay awake, staring at the ceiling.

The next day, after her weekly appointment with her psychiatrist, Catherine had met Nina for lunch. Their favorite restaurant, Le Dernier Mot, was on Newbury Street and their favorite lunch was watercress salad and shrimp. Normally, they shared their latest political, as well as social, plans which included the fact that Catherine was attending less and less of Daniel's and his mother's events. Catherine was wearing dark glasses because her eyes were red from crying.

When they hugged, Nina held her away and looked at her quizzically. "What's the matter, Catherine?"

Catherine's tears ran down her cheeks as she told Nina. There was no way she could be involved in the antiwar demonstrations any more. She felt strongly about the war needing to end, about our troops needing to come home, and she believed in peaceful protest, but the cost to her marriage was too dear. The peace vigils, the requests to meet with Senators to pull the troops out of Vietnam, it all had to stop. Daniel was too angered by it.

Nina was incensed. "How can you let your husband tell you what to do? If Barry every spoke to me like that..."

Catherine leaned forward, not wanting to be heard by other people at nearby tables. Nina did the same. In a near whisper, filled with emotion, Catherine had to say out loud what was racing around in her head.

"When we argued last night and I said maybe we shouldn't be together, Daniel got so angry! He said he could have me committed![7] He said I would never see my children again! I think my psychiatrist agrees with him. Dr. Bernstein thinks I am wrong to want to do things other than support my husband while he is building his career. He says my job is to take care of our children and our home. I'm afraid, Nina, I don't want to lose my children."

In her meeting with her psychiatrist, he had sided with her husband again. Dr. Bernstein had told her in no uncertain terms that if he were her husband, he would be angry, too.

"Your job is to be a good wife to your husband and a good mother to your children!" Dr. Bernstein had said.

Catherine had looked down at her hands. She felt ashamed as well as miserable. "But, I would like to have a career, too," she replied, perhaps sounding a bit petulant.

"Just support your husband, that's enough to do with an infant and a toddler." Dr. Bernstein sounded angry with her, and Catherine began to cry.

He changed her medication. It would take a long time—moving to Vermont, in fact—before she was able to finally flush the pills down the toilet.

Those days were so hard, she had no idea it could get worse as time moved forward. She thought moving to Vermont would fix everything. She could picture it all in her mind. *A new beginning. A fresh start.* They would find their way back to each other.

She took Laura and Becky for a walk down the dirt road and they would explore something new each day. One way the road went past the little cemetery with old headstones. They read the names and some of the dates meant that they were only two or three years old.

"Why are there so many little children?" asked Laura.

"Because that was before they had vaccinations against all of the bad diseases."

"I hate vax-vax-natins," said Becky.

"I know, but those shots protect you, sweetie. My mom nearly died as a child from scarlet fever and now we don't have scarlet fever anymore. And, polio used to cripple children, but you are also protected from ever getting polio."

"What's cripple?"

"It's like being injured, like having a broken arm or leg, only it never gets better."

On the weekends, she and Daniel took their daughters on picnics and walked down the long road together enjoying the grandeur of the old maples which made a leafy roof overhead. Nearby, a small lake with a sandy beach was perfect for a swim on a hot, summer's day.

And, during the week, Catherine would take short hikes with the girls on old logging roads to explore the land. Sometimes, the trees parted and there were views where they could see mountains off in the distance. Catherine showed them wild flowers that she remembered from her summers in the country. Delightedly, she pointed them out, "Look girls, look at the lady slippers! And over there, trillium! Aren't they beautiful?"

The girls crouched down and peered closely at the flowers. They knew they could not pick them as they were too rare. Once, they came across a jack-in-the-pulpit.

"I wish they grew around our house," said Laura.

"Me, too," copied Becky.

"Wouldn't that be something? I wonder if there are any wildflowers in the back meadows."

"Can we go to the lake now?" asked Becky.

"Let's go later when it's not so crowded," answered Catherine. "I also need to draw up some plans for our family room and for some changes in the main rooms we need."

"You spend an awful lot of time drawing," said Laura.

"I know, honey, but I just want to get it all done before Labor Day when we have to return to Boston."

It was time to leave the old logging road and walk up the dirt road to the farmhouse. Catherine looked forward each day to her task of sketching on the large sheets of floor plans to arrange furniture and get a feel for how it would look once the renovations were finished. She tried to get the girls involved, showing them the arrangement of each room and the scaled-to-size furniture, but they preferred to use the large sheets of paper to draw on with crayons. They drew trees, flowers and lots of green for grass to create pictures of their new surroundings.

One weekend, Daniel brought up a letter from home. Their nanny, Anna, had written to say that she would be back in September but not till the end. Her father had taken ill and she was needed at home. Laura and Becky wanted to know if that was a long time.

"Not too long," answered Daniel. "But we need her so your mother can go to the charity events with Grammy. It helps people who aren't as fortunate as we are."

"Why aren't they as fortunate as we are?" asked Laura.

"Because they don't have the money we have."

Catherine winced.

When Daniel had finally approved of Catherine's desire to build a family room by renovating the connecting shed between the house and barn, the project had provided her with a focus which she found exciting, and a replacement for the work as an interior designer she had given up in order to make her marriage better.

Little did Catherine realize that the family room would be the straw that broke the camel's back. As the summer wore on, her obsession with the family room grew. She could barely sleep at night, so filled with ideas and previews of things to come in her mind—and she became determined to stay at the farm until everything was completed. It was later, when August came, that the thread of an idea of living there full-time began to take hold.

The outside of the farmhouse looked perfectly traditional, just the way Catherine wanted it to be, while the inside had been transformed with a couple of the sculpted pieces and a few of the contemporary oil paintings Daniel brought up from Boston. The plaster walls were painted a pale, pearl gray to act as a neutral background that would be better for displaying the kind of art work Daniel preferred.

The need to insulate the house had closed off the exposed wood beams, and there was a general feel of sterility when they first moved in. Daniel liked it that way, but Catherine had other ideas about making it feel warmer by finding soft fabrics that would pick up some of the colors in the paintings. She could create a theme for each room. There was nothing she could do about the clanking copper bush that Daniel thought was beautiful, so she set it outside in the shrubbery that lined the front of the house. She also placed a concrete owl to the side of the front porch, hoping it wasn't too noticeable from the road. The renovations went on and on. The trucks kept coming and going.

Catherine had to tangle with the work men a few times. She had asked, specifically, that they "maintain the integrity of the original interior"—particularly when installing wood framing and a door that would lead into the barn. The old entry door from the shed was made of planks and had more spaces than wood, but there were old doors with the same wrought iron latches as the rest of the house piled up on the second floor in the barn.

Unbeknownst to Catherine, the work men had cleaned out the barn and taken all the old doors to the dump. There were other items that may have been missing, but Daniel wanted everything removed. He couldn't tolerate clutter of any kind.

When she found out, she went ballistic.

Every weekend when her husband arrived, so would Jack, the owner of Richardson's Carpentry. At that time, they would converse about the progress. The fireplace in the new family room took a long time, as expected, but the walls were insulated and plastered leaving the ceiling beams exposed as Catherine requested. They had had to refit the floor boards of the overhead loft, and put a railing around it for safety's sake. The only way to get to it was with a ladder.

One afternoon during the week, Catherine decided to see how things were coming along. The work men had their saw horses in the middle of the room on the unfinished flooring. The fresh scent of sawn wood filled the air as they were cutting boards for the far end of the room that would cover the insulation and finish the last wall.

However, at the end of the room for the new entry into the barn was a hollow core door.

Catherine's mouth dropped open when she saw it.

"What is that?" she pointed.

The foreman, whom Catherine didn't know, said, "That's the new door from the family room into the barn."

"No, oh no, absolutely not! I specifically told Mr. Richards that we had an old pile of doors in the barn with the latches on them!"

"Well, they are a different size and don't fit into the frame."

"Then fix the frame, make it fit, and put in a matching door. It doesn't make any sense to see such a door when every single one in the entire house is made with four panels, and has the wrought iron latch on it."

"Ahhhh, I think they were taken to the dump."

"What? With all the hardware on them? Then you will have to go get them!"

"That's going to take more time, I think I should ask your husband, and it's going to cost more money...."

Catherine spoke carefully, enunciating each word evenly. "Let me get this straight. Without asking either my husband or me, you took the doors to the dump?"

"Well, yes, your husband wanted the second floor cleaned out....."

"My husband appointed me to oversee this project and I am an interior designer by trade. Go and retrieve those doors and put them back in the barn. Then, change the frame to fit the door that will match the rest of the doors in the house, and install the best one. Thank you!"

Catherine spun on her heel, gritting her teeth and went inside the kitchen hallway, slamming the door behind her.

Two of the work men looked at the foreman. "Guess we better go back to the dump."

Catherine invited her former boss, Albert Greenshaw, from Boston to drive up for a weekend to help her with figuring out what she needed. She also wanted to get Albert's point of view, and see if he could envision it the way she did.

Usually, Catherine would drive the children to their riding lessons dressed in their jodhpurs and black hats, but she needed every moment to work with Albert on the house plans, as he could only spare Saturday, returning to Boston Sunday. She hoped to make enough decisions that Albert would be willing to do some of the ordering of fabrics and wallpaper for her. She had called Mr. Bell and put Albert up in town at the local inn, knowing it wouldn't be to his liking. She knew how fussy he was. She warned him about the casual country attire and the stages of work going on at the farm, but he had brushed her words aside. *Oh Albert! Will you show up in your sport coat and ascot with your distinguished-looking hair all styled into place?* Catherine chuckled.

Labor Day weekend kept feeling closer, and since it was already July, Catherine wanted to get as much completed as possible. She knew it would take weeks to get any fabric or wallpaper delivered that she ordered.

She would ask Daniel as soon as they had had dinner Friday evening if he would take the girls to their lessons on Saturday.

At the table in the dining room, Daniel sat at the head and Laura and Becky sat side-by-side. Catherine sat closest to the kitchen so she could get up when anything was needed.

Daniel looked at the plate. "What is that?"

"Rice and broccoli with crab cakes."

"It's all brown."

"Yes, the rice is brown and I did cook the crab cakes too long, but I got it at the High Health Food Store in town."

"You mean where all the hippies go?"

"There aren't any hippies around here. What are you talking about? Brown rice is a healthy grain—white rice is bleached and you might as well eat library paste."

"I was raised with white rice. I like white rice."

"Okay, okay, I will make you some instant, bleached, no-nutritional-value white rice." Catherine got up from the table and put the water on to boil on the electric stove top. It was too warm to build a fire in the little wood cook stove, and she really didn't know how to build a fire anyway.

Laura and Becky tried a few bites and pushed their food around their plates while their mother banged pots and pans in the kitchen.

"The crab cakes taste all right," said Daniel, "eat your crab cakes, girls, they're fine."

"Good to know," muttered Catherine.

By the time the white rice was ready, the girls were finished with whatever they had eaten.

"We're done, Mommy," said Laura.

"All right, you can leave the table."

The girls went off to the parlor to try to find a television station they could watch. Sometimes they received reception, but most of the time it was too snowy to see anything. They had their dolls and little doll furniture in the parlor, as well as all their large, wooden building blocks. They never tired of making a doll house out of the blocks.

"Daniel, Albert is coming up Saturday to help me with some paint and wallpaper decisions for the house. Would you please take Laura and Becky to their riding lessons?"

She had kept up their riding lessons as they would be outside in beautiful meadows, but felt that they deserved a summer off from piano and ballet. The stables were an equestrian's dream: riding arenas set in lush fields with a rolling backdrop of green, peaked mountains.

"Sure, I can do that. I would rather spend time with the girls anyway."

Daniel decided to take his daughters out to lunch after their lessons. Then they could go to some of the interesting shops in the village. *The last thing I need is spending time with Albert*, Daniel thought. *What a pretentious jerk.* He didn't like the way Albert flounced around like he was sniffing something unappealing and the way he dressed—effeminate scarves instead of men's ties. Daniel found that loathsome. Even worse was the way he seemed to look down his nose at Daniel—when Albert was about a foot shorter! He thought it was Albert's fault that Catherine had tried to go back to work and that he had filled her head with foolish ideas.

By taking his daughters to their riding lessons and out for lunch, it would lessen the chance of spending any time around Albert. *I hope by the time we get back, he'll be gone.* The girls could change at the stables and with that in mind, he went upstairs and grabbed a pair of jeans and sneakers for each one.

They could also go to that terrific hardware store that carried all sorts of tools and items which he could endlessly browse. He never knew what he would come upon at Caruthers' Brothers store. The girls loved to go there because of the main attraction, Fred the cat. He was a giant-sized calico who slept in the storefront window. The first time they saw the cat, he was so enormous, they didn't think he was real. They learned that he weighed 44 pounds. The owner, a dapper gentleman named Mr. Caruthers, who always wore red suspenders, had told them jokingly that the cat was as much the reason for his store's success as the array of hard-to-find and no-longer-made odd tools and items.

Rebecca, with her dark brown hair in braids, wanted to see Fred after her riding lessons.

"After lunch, Becky, then we'll visit Fred," Daniel said as he smiled at his girls. They had lunch at their favorite ice cream and sandwich shop, and then walked across the street to the store where Fred lounged in the store front window.

As soon as they went inside, Rebecca reached into the store window and touched the cat's fur.

"Don't!" said Laura, the wise six-year-old, tossing her blonde hair in a way that reminded Daniel of Catherine. "Daddy! Look at what Rebecca is doing! She's touching Fred!"

"It's okay, Laura," said Daniel smiling.

The cat moved his enormous head toward Becky and she involuntarily jumped back. In one turn of his huge bulk, he rolled onto his back with paws up, unearthing a pile of cedar shavings mixed with clumps of cat hair.

"He wants you to rub his belly," Daniel said.

Becky looked up at her dad and wrinkled her nose. "He smells funny, Daddy," she replied.

"It's probably the cedar. Don't you want to pet his fur?" her father asked.

"I will!" said Laura, who reached into the window and patted the cat gently. He just lolled there in the sun with his eyes shut, purring.

As the sun glinted off the glass, Daniel caught the reflection of himself with his two daughters sharing a rare moment together. Daniel wondered what was happening to his carefully planned life, his marriage and the ideas he held for the future of his wife and family. He knew what was best and felt he couldn't let anything stand in the way of his vision. His wife was becoming increasingly difficult, picking up the radical ideas of the times. *But,* Daniel thought, *this will pass just like all the other things of interest she has picked up and put down. That's it; this will all blow over in time.*

The girls followed Daniel around the store, and enjoyed looking at the various old metal tools that were displayed on the walls. Mr. Caruthers came over to explain the tools to the children, but he knew from the expression on Daniel Janson's face that he wasn't familiar with any of these tools either.

"So Daniel, can I help you find a tool you might need for the farm?" Mr. Caruthers asked.

"No, no, Mr. Caruthers, I'm not good at using tools and I know it."

"Well, then, who fixes things in your house?"

"I'm just one of those city folks who keep lots of people employed!" laughed Daniel.

"Touché," said Mr. Caruthers with a wry smile. He knew he had better quit while he was at least even. Daniel had no illusions about being one of those who fix their own things. While Mr. Caruthers had been running the store for twenty years, he had inherited it from his family and had left New York City at age 40 to take it over. He had learned to chide out-of-town customers, referred to as 'flatlanders,' in his best Vermont-adopted accent. He had taken enough teasing from the 'real' Vermonters who were born and lived there all their lives to know how to do it. He wondered about the Jansons and what they would come to learn while living in the country as summer people.

Albert had marked a red line on his car map of the state of Vermont and followed it up Route 93 to Interstate 89 in his old, silver Mercedes.

"So far, so good," he said aloud while casting an eye to the map as it lay open on the passenger seat. When he took the exit, it wasn't long before the road turned to dirt.

This is unusual, Albert thought, as he slowed down to keep from banging up his car as it careened unevenly over the dirt roads. He remembered Catherine had said it would be about ten miles from the highway to her "fabulous country setting." *Fabulous, indeed.* There were no other houses on the road—unbelievable—except the one he was to find before hers.

She had said the farmhouse was about a mile or two beyond an 1800's Cape Cod style house. "You can't miss it," she told him. "The mailbox by the Cape has giant capital letters painted on it, 'WAINWRIGHT' – just keep going up the hill."

There were no signs. There was nothing but trees for as far as the eye could see. "What the hell?" he said aloud. "What could Catherine be thinking moving to this godforsaken place in the middle of nowhere?" Finally, he spotted the old Cape with the mailbox on the side of the road. As his car began to climb the hill, he knew he had found it somehow.

Catherine heard the diesel engine moan and came out on the front porch to greet Albert. There were trucks parked all over the side yard and piles of boards and concrete blocks strewn every which way. As Albert got out of his car, he grabbed his weathered leather carrying case and headed toward the front porch, yelling out, "Good grief, Catherine! What have you gotten yourself into this time?"

God only knows, Catherine thought to herself as she smiled, covering her discomfort. She had known Albert all through college when she had become an apprentice to him, and he gave her her first job upon graduation. He was very successful and very particular—she really had to step it up a notch to keep in his good graces. Whenever she worked on his projects, he questioned every little thing she wanted to do. As Catherine learned over time, it was Albert's interest in how people arrived at their decisions. He had questioned her marriage. He had questioned her pregnancies. When she returned to work for him, and it didn't work out, he had questioned her marriage again. And now, he could add this to his list of questions that she knew would be forthcoming.

Catherine greeted Albert with a big hug, and taking his arm, ushered him into the kitchen.

"Sit down! I have just the tonic for your long drive!" Catherine said, and poured a steaming mug of coffee, rich and dark, just the way he liked it.

"Where's the coffee cups?" Albert asked.

"Mugs at the farm!" Catherine replied.

"What about that fine bone china?"

"Oh, please, Albert! Lighten up! It's the country. I came here to get away from your wicked city ways!" Catherine responded, laughingly.

"Humpf." Albert sniffed. "I fail to see the reason to leave a little city like Boston under any circumstances. First you leave your career, and then you leave a proper life. What next? I suppose you'll start wearing—" Albert paused as he examined Catherine's outfit and realized she was wearing blue jeans. "Blue jeans!"

"And you are dressed to perfection as you usually are," offered Catherine, trying to stay in his good graces.

She picked up the tube on the table and unrolled the sketches of the family room. Albert grinned.

As she spread out the large pages, the sound of hammering clearly entered the kitchen.

"What is that racket?" asked Albert.

"It's the workmen putting together the family room. That's why I need your help, Albert. I have these ideas about fabrics with textures, and some of the complementary paint colors for the family room. You are so good at pulling these things together and I did want you to see this dear, old place."

"I can't think with all this noise! Is there a quiet place we can go?"

"Sure, we can go to Daniel's study—it's not furnished yet but there are enough chairs and a table for us two."

On the other side of the house, with very little furniture was an old parlor Catherine planned to turn into

Daniel's study. It held a table, a desk and two chairs. The arched fireplace with the classic mantel gave the room a warm appeal. The beauty of the old house was that there were doors to every room, so Catherine closed the kitchen hall door that would eventually lead into the family room. She gestured to Albert to follow her, and they went through the kitchen to the dining room where another door could be closed, then to the furthest room away from the noise. Once they entered the room and shut the door, the din of hammers was lessened to a distant, resounding rhythm.

After they got settled, their heads leaning over the drawings like old times, Catherine realized how much she missed working with Albert.

"Are you happy, Catherine?" Albert asked, out of the blue.

"Oh, Albert. Let's not talk about happiness now. We don't have that much time. I need to focus on getting this done."

"Catherine, I've known you since you were fresh out of college. I know when something is up. If you don't want to talk now, promise me you will when you return in September."

"Okay, Albert, I promise," Catherine said, meeting his eyes and raising her hands out in front of her. "But for now, please, please help me get to the end of this."

"Okay." Albert gave her a stern look. "But, I will hold you to that conversation."

"All right, Albert. All right."

Catherine stood up and stretched.

"Come on, let's do a walk-through of the house so you can get a feel for it." Catherine suggested.

They went up the front staircase, climbing the narrow pine stairs with care. Then, through the bedrooms and bathroom upstairs, ("Only one *full* bathroom!" said Albert, shocked) down the back staircase, and into the noisy hall. Then, back to the study. After an hour of looking at samples of fabrics and color slides Albert had brought, Catherine thought she'd surprise Albert with a 'civilized' lunch.

"I went to the next town for pate de fois gras, crusty French bread, sweet pickles, and Grey Poupon—just for you Albert!" It was an old joke between them that Albert dined regularly on French food and that a good pate was one of his favorite meals. "I'll bring a tray into the study. Will that suit you?" Catherine said with a twinkle in her eye.

Albert was glad to see her looking less pensive and smiled broadly.

"I am obliged to you, dear lady, just remember to bring dinner napkins of the cloth variety and a dry, white burgundy to go with."

"Of course, my liege!" Catherine said, sweeping her arm down in front of her in a mock bow.

Catherine smiled as she went to the kitchen to prepare the tray. She hadn't enjoyed herself so much for some time, not realizing it until this visit from her former boss, then colleague, now friend. She wondered where she was headed as she could see that her feelings about her life recently weren't usually this pleasant. Pushing her questions aside, she stayed with the lunch plan, and was glad she had some of the large, cloth, dinner napkins kept clean in a plastic bag. The dust from the family room project filtered into the kitchen lightly covering everything.

"Voila!" Catherine said as she returned to the study, even managing a fresh flower on the tray from the wild gardens around the front porch.

Albert clapped his hands together. "Lovely! Oh, Catherine, you are such a darling!"

With the fine crystal and a few good plates, Albert was pleased. Everything was arranged so nicely, it was hard to believe they were in this old house in Vermont. As they enjoyed their lunch, Albert was amazed that Catherine had been able to find good pate in the area.

"Oh Albert! You act like you've stepped into a time warp! I do have to drive to another town, but you can get the same good things here!"

"Thank heavens for that. Otherwise, dear girl, I don't know how you would survive."

By the afternoon, they were both tired and Catherine offered to have Albert follow her to town to find the local inn. Albert said not to worry. He had seen it on his way in—what he didn't say was that there was no way in hell he was staying there overnight.

They said their goodbyes, and Albert left knowing he had a long drive ahead of him until he reached civilization.

Daniel and the girls arrived in time for the dinner that Catherine was preparing on the wood cook stove. It had taken her a few times to figure out how to open the damper and make the fire just right, but she seemed to have gotten the hang of it. The remnants of the pate were gone; the tray put away, the cloth napkins in the laundry. Daniel spotted the white burgundy bottle in the fridge.

"Drinking on the job?" he asked.

"With Albert? Of course!"

"So, it went well?"

"Yes, I needed less input than I thought I did, but his help with colors, fabrics and wallpaper was great. Once the family room is done, I think much of the finishing will be fairly straightforward."

"That's good news because it's time to trade the cars in, so the less additional expenses than planned on, the better. Do you want another Volvo?"

"Gee, no, Daniel. I think I need a Jeep with four-wheel-drive."

"Why? A Volvo is a good, safe car for you and the girls."

"I know, but what if we decide to come up in the winter?"

"What for? Why would we? This is a summer home, nothing more."

"Okay, but just say we did—would you want to take a chance on coming up these roads in a regular car? And, what about last winter when the city closed down because of a snowstorm? We couldn't go anywhere because of the roads."

"All right, maybe you're right about that. A Jeep it is."

Daniel went upstairs to wash up and change for dinner, and Laura and Rebecca chatted nonstop about their entire day, moment to moment. As Catherine looked into their eyes with their earnest expressions, she wondered if she was doing what was best for them. *What if we can't find a way to bridge our differences*? The growing chasm between her and Daniel hadn't gotten any smaller. Anxious thoughts swirled around her mind. *What if returning to Boston made things worse than they were? Would a little separation help us see things differently? And then, what if Daniel could have me institutionalized and take my girls?*

Catherine tried to stay in the moment with her daughters and take part in their enthusiasm and child-sweet conversation.

FALL 1974

How can people be so heartless?
How can people by so cruel?
Easy to be hard, easy to be cold...

James Rado, Gerome Ragni and Galt MacDermot,

"Easy To Be Hard," *Hair, Off Broadway Musical*, 1967

Chapter 3

As August neared its end, the family room was almost finished. Daniel slept in the bedroom overlooking the meadow and Catherine had moved to the low-ceilinged guest room in the front of the house, saying she couldn't sleep at night. She loved how that room had turned out. It was covered with wallpaper that made the room look like you had stepped into a garden. The old, wood floor boards that weren't beautiful like the wide, pine boards on the first floor, looked perfect painted white. The flowery printed sheets had the same color tones as the wallpaper, and were complementary under a snowy white bed cover from Germany. Every time she entered the room, she knew it was meant for her.

By the time they were to pack up their belongings, the weekend before Labor Day, Catherine had made up her mind to put Laura into school in town and find a kindergarten for Becky. She took them to the Town Clerk's office to register, and talked to them about it during the week when Daniel was in Boston. Upon his return, she decided to tell him as soon as he arrived and get it over with. *How can I be both excited and frightened at the same time,* she thought. *Daniel will be furious with me! But, maybe if I explain it right, he will understand. Maybe if we came down during school vacations and long weekends. Maybe...*

Catherine prepared Daniel's favorite food: steak and potatoes. She also made a large mixed salad with carrots, just the way he liked it. He loathed tomatoes so she put some sliced ones on the side for her and her girls.

It was such lovely weather that the girls ran back outside to play as soon as they finished eating. In the little front yard which was fenced off from all the work men's piles of rubble, they had a cedar log swing that they could both sit in and enjoy. Catherine looked out the window, assuring herself where Laura and Becky were, then returned to the dining room table.

"I've been thinking about the unfinished family room and I want to stay here, Daniel. I want to stay longer and see it through."

"Wha-a-at? What are you talking about?" said Daniel. "We agreed that this is to be our summer home. That's it. A summer home."

"I want to live here year round and have the girls go to school here—just try it for one year. You can come up weekends, like you do now; it won't be all that different. During the week you are hardly ever home before the girls go to bed—"

"That's not the same! We have a life there!"

"You have a life there! You're the big deal! I want a life! And I want a better life for the girls than all that phony-baloney stuff we have to do socially for your career!"

"You don't know what's best for our girls!"

"And you do when you are never home?!"

Daniel's voice rose further, "I've had about enough, Catherine!" He pounded his fist on the kitchen counter.

The screen door slammed. The girls could hear them arguing outside.

"Mommy, Daddy, what are you doing?" said Laura as she came into the kitchen, her eyes big and questioning.

"I'm sorry, honey," said Catherine.

Becky walked in crying.

"What's the matter, Becky?"

"You and daddy are mad."

"Nice going, Catherine."

Catherine just looked at Daniel as she held Becky on her lap.

After awhile, she walked them into the living room to play with their dolls, and once they were settled, she returned to the kitchen.

Softly, she began, "I'm not happy, Daniel, I don't know what I want anymore."

"Happy? Who said you are supposed to be happy? You're a wife and mother with responsibilities and that's life. It's not about whether you are happy or not."

"Are you happy Daniel?"

"I don't think about it. I just go to work and take care of my family. That's my life. That's how it is."

As they seemed to have reached an impasse, Catherine checked the fire in the wood stove. Daniel went to the refrigerator, turned to Catherine and said, "We're out of milk. Go to the store and get it, will you, Catherine? After all, I've just driven almost three hours to get here."

The nearest little store was at least twenty minutes away, by the gas station, miles from Old Sheldon Road. Catherine was annoyed but acquiesced since she was doing all the demanding of late.

What happened next shook her to her roots. Upon her return, Daniel's car was gone. She knew immediately he had taken her daughters. She had stopped the Jeep and stood in the middle of the road, wailing like an animal, and fell to her knees. She was pounding in the dirt yelling, "No! No!" until a kindly distant neighbor, Jed Bishop, came along, and stopped his truck. He opened the truck door, jumped down and came over to her.

"Catherine, what's wrong? What's happened?"

Jed reached down to Catherine, pulled her to her feet, and carefully walked her up the front porch stairs into the house.

Her world had split into a million kaleidoscopic pieces. She thought her heart would stop beating. "He took my girls! He took them!"

"Who took them?"

"Daniel!!"

"Why do you think he took them? Maybe they just went to the store..."

"He sent me to the store! He sent me!!"

Jed looked around the parlor and led Catherine to the rocking chair. "Sit, sit. Do you have any beer in the fridge?"

"No, no, Daniel doesn't drink beer."

"How about some scotch or bourbon? Gin?"

"No, we never have any hard liquor."

"You need a good shot of something strong right now."

Jed had been welcoming to her and her daughters when they first arrived. He had invited them all to his farm, taking great care to explain things in response to her girls' many questions.

He asked her who she could call. He walked with her to the hall that led to the shed by the back staircase where the only telephone was on the wall. She called Albert and told him what had happened.

"Get a lawyer fast! I mean right now!!" Albert said.

"I—I don't know any lawyers here."

"I do," said Jed, standing nearby.

When she got off the phone, Jed was standing next to her, watching her with his big brown eyes, his baseball cap in his hands.

"I'll need a tough one."

"I know one; he's supposed to be really good."

He gave her a name to look up in the phone book, and said he had to do an errand, but he'd be right back.

She called the lawyer's home phone. When he answered, she began to explain why she was calling and just broke down. Through shaking sobs, she told him what had happened.

"I can call the State Police and have him picked up."

"No, no, it would frighten the children. They wouldn't understand."

"All right. Stay put there, and call your family. Get some support around you." He would see her on Monday in his office.

She really didn't want to call her mother.

"Hi, Mom?"

"What's wrong?"

"Everything, everything is wrong," sobbed Catherine.

By the time she was off the phone with her mother, Jed had returned with a pizza and a six-pack of beer. "You need to eat some pizza for your stomach and then you need to put away this six-pack."

Catherine just stared at him. He sat her down on the sofa in the front room and opened the pizza box, pulled out a slice and handed it to her.

"I'm not hungry."

"Eat it."

Catherine took a few bites. Jed took out a knife and flipped off the beer cap.

"Take a drink."

"I don't want any."

"You really need to drink this, and you have to trust me about it right now. You need this in your system. Otherwise, I will have to take you to the hospital."

What she didn't know was that her face looked ashen, and appeared stone-like. Jed was afraid she was going into shock. He thought the alcohol would help, perhaps have a calming effect.

The next day when her mother arrived, she took one look at her, and asked for the phone book. Her father got back in the car and drove her to the emergency room at the nearest hospital. At first, the doctor had thought she had suffered a small stroke. She could still remember the pained expression on her mother's face, mirroring her own, knowing that something was terribly wrong.

The vivid pain of loss, of not knowing if she would get her daughters back, of never feeling she could trust Daniel again became the dark rhythm of her life. Deep underneath was a river of cold, black fear.

On Monday, her father called Attorney Farley and said that Catherine would have to come the following week—she was too distraught right now. Her mother would stay on, but would need to return home in a few days to pack some things for the longer time she planned to be there to care for her. Catherine neither ate nor slept the first week. Her mother led her to the table for three meals a day until she began to eat again, and to wake her up the same time every morning so she could re-establish a routine.

"That's it, pick up the fork. Atta girl, take another bite." Everything seemed filtered through a hazy, nebulous atmosphere, as if she was losing her vision.

Her mother closed the girls' bedroom doors so that every time Catherine walked by she wouldn't be constantly reminded of their emptiness. Her dad would have to return to his classes during each week, but would drive up weekends, and talk with her attorney if need be.

Catherine kept saying to her mother, over and over, "Not one thing of my girls is left, not one thing! Not a sock! Not even a sock!"

At different times, when her mother was busy in the kitchen, Catherine would sneak into Laura's and Becky's rooms and smell the pillows on their beds for a sense of their presence. She refused to let her mother wash their sheets. She kept asking herself, *What if this is all I have to remember them by?* Fresh tears would begin anew.

After the first two weeks, she had to drive herself to meet with her attorney alone. Her mother and dad had returned home for a few days to take care of things in their lives that had been interrupted by this unplanned-for event.

I should drive again, she thought. I need to get myself on an even keel. Maybe driving will make me feel stronger.

It was a cold, rainy day and the offices were actually quite a distance outside of Montpelier. She found the road through the pouring rain. The offices were in a gambrel-roofed building with barn board and window boxes. I *must be in the wrong place*, she thought. A meadow opened up behind the building, and the parking lot to the right was arranged with cars lined up beside a typical farm fence. Catherine didn't know what she expected from the supposedly toughest attorney in the state, but certainly *not* this setting.

Once in his presence, however, she felt a vibration that seemed to generate from him in waves as he spoke. He was certain about what he was saying, and exuded a confidence that she couldn't even imagine attaining for herself. He paced around his office while talking nonstop about his plans for the case.

"You have to get your children back, get a job in your town, and carry on your life as a stable, conscious, mother. Then, we'll build the evidence for your case, reams of paper that will stack up to the windowsills..."

He was totally committed to seeing her have her children, be divorced and get on with her life. That was all she was sure he was telling her, but that was all she wanted, although she was still viewing life through a tear-soaked blur.

Attorney Farley had asked her to get a mental health evaluation—as an outpatient. He wanted to be able to have a rebuttal prepared for Daniel's accusations.

She made an appointment to see a psychiatrist, Dr. Lindberg, who was affiliated with the area's hospital and she was to go regularly until the divorce was settled.

Her new psychiatrist said that her husband was a controlling bully and that she had to learn to stand on her own two feet.

After her mom and dad returned, she explained the plans of her attorney to have regular meetings. Her mom would be there during the week to drive her if necessary.

For the next few weeks, she met with her psychiatrist and her attorney to be prepared for the depositions that Daniel's lawyers kept postponing. Finally, she had been able to not burst into tears at any questions about her children. The rehearsals were making her stronger, which in retrospect must have been her attorney's intention. After one such meeting, Attorney Farley had delivered a pep talk, of sorts.

"You have to be strong! You can't just fall apart every time someone talks to you about your children. They'll think you are either hiding something or unable to deal with difficult times! You can't give that appearance!" he yelled.

"But I haven't always been a good mother, I've lost my temper at my children, I've spanked them and yelled at them, and I tried to go back to work when the youngest was still a baby," said Catherine.

"Big deal! This isn't about being Mother Teresa! This is about real life! People lose their tempers! Mothers go to work! My mother worked at a time when it was totally not done. 'You have to live your life as if it's the only one you have—because it is!' she used to say to my brother and me. When my father died in World War II, my mother supported our family all by herself. And, told us about the women who flew planes in World War II that were never talked about. She made us believe we could do anything we wanted to do—and so can you! This is your life, Catherine! It's all you have! Are you going to live it for yourself or under some antiquated societal rules with a dictator for a husband?"

Her attorney had stormed around his office, yelling at her for doubting herself. His tie went askew, his shirt became rumpled, and a sheen of oil glistened on his forehead with agitation.

Catherine was shocked by the exchange. Her attorney was the first person in her life that acted as if her desires and dreams were normal. Not even her parents had supported her in her wishes. She could remember her mother's response when she told her that she didn't think her marriage was working. Her mother had instructed her to "tough it out"—however, she no longer maintained that position.

The legal battle raged on over who would have custody of the children. When her attorney was instructed by Daniel's attorneys to bring up reconciliation, Catherine had laughed out loud. Daniel's betrayal made reconciliation impossible. She would never, could never, trust him again.

First, the fighting over who would have the children to raise. Then, the knowledge that she would have to face depositions questioning her mental stability. It was an underlying stream that threatened to toss her off balance— she knew not when.

She had chosen Attorney Farley because he had a reputation for wearing down his opponents. In his entire career as a Vermont attorney, he had only lost one case in court and it was said that that was a fluke. Fluke or not, after her neighbor, Jed had found her in the road that fateful night and recommended him, she had asked other people in the town about Attorney Farley. His legal skills had come highly recommended; and, she had to get her children back.

Daniel was surprised and angry at her for having gotten a lawyer as quickly as she had. He called her often, but when she would pick up the phone and hear it was him, she hung up.

Daniel called one night after her parents returned. Her father had answered the phone and wouldn't let him talk to her. She had only heard one side of the conversation, but her father was as angry as any time she had ever seen him in her life—squared. "You rotten bastard! You took those little girls knowing how it would hurt Catherine! I'd like to beat the living daylights out of you!"

Her father later told her that Daniel said he just took them to visit their grandparents.

That's when she heard him reply:

"And all their clothes and shoes?"

Supposedly, Catherine had hurt Daniel by taking steps on her own, by not believing it would work itself out. She was less convinced that she could live her life with any semblance of herself as long as she had to report to a husband. After all, Daniel had done the unforgivable.

One Friday night, around 6:00 PM, the phone rang. Her father had just arrived from Boston and was walking through the front door as Catherine was speaking to Attorney Farley.

The girls would be returned tomorrow to live with her while they worked out the details, and Daniel would drive halfway to meet her.

She collapsed into her mother's arms.

"I can't do it! I can't meet Daniel!"

"I'll drive back to meet him, I'll get them," said her dad.

"Oh, would you? Would you, Daddy?"

She ran into his bear hug, unable to stop the flow of tears.

In the morning, Catherine stood at the window in the parlor, gazing down the snow-covered road.

"Honey, it's going to take at least four hours for Daddy to go to meet Daniel, and drive all the way back. Even halfway on these wintry roads is going to make driving slow."

"I know, I know. I can hardly stand the wait."

"You need to pull yourself together for the girls, you know, they must be pretty confused by now."

"I will."

Catherine went into the downstairs bathroom, smoothed her hair, and splashed her face with cold water. Her red-rimmed eyes were the only sign of her prolonged grief.

After what seemed like days, she heard her father's car climbing the hill. She ran out the front door, onto the porch. Then, unable to keep from running, she slid on the front walk, catching herself as she came to the car door.

"Mommy! Mommy!" she heard her daughters cry out before the door was even opened. She pulled open the car door, and Laura and Becky fell into her arms. She drew them in to her and held them as close as she could over their winter hats and coats.

Her dad walked around the car toward her and her eyes filled, "Thank you, Daddy."

He nodded as he blinked back the tears watching his daughter's reunion with her girls.

"I've got to unload the trunk," her dad said, "I have quite a lot of boxes and bags."

Her mother came to the door with a coat on to help her husband bring everything into the house. The girls hugged her.

"You go inside now, it's too cold out here. You, too, Catherine, you have a lot of catching up to do."

They walked into the front entry and began taking off their boots. Catherine hung their coats in the closet under the stairs, and brought the girls into the kitchen to make them cocoa.

"Are Grandma and Grandpa living with us?" asked Laura.

"No, honey, they are just visiting for awhile."

"I like being with Grammy and Papa in Boston."

"That's nice," answered Catherine.

"I missed you, Mommy," said Becky, crawling into her lap.

Every time she looked at her girls, she cried. Laura and Becky were glad to be back, but her crying upset them. Her mother called her sisters, and two days later they appeared with their children to visit and offer support. The girls were glad for the activity, and it helped Catherine begin to heal from the traumatic event.

Everyone left a few days later, and Catherine was alone with Laura and Becky, getting them acclimated into their new school.

In November, as it neared Thanksgiving, Attorney Farley called to say she could keep the girls this year for the Thanksgiving holiday. The relief was followed by her fear that she couldn't put together a real dinner. She called her parents as she had been warned against leaving Vermont in case Daniel planned to try to throw the divorce into Massachusetts. Her mother said that they would bring everything, not to do anything whatsoever.

"Cranberry sauce?"

"Even cranberry sauce—not to worry. It will be fine."

Catherine was glad since she wasn't sure of her ability to do justice to what used to be one of her favorite holidays.

It had already snowed that week when she was driving the girls to town for Becky's morning kindergarten and Laura's first grade. The closest school bus would drop Laura off a mile away, so she felt compelled to drive to town twice each day. When she picked up Becky at noon, they would go to Whitey's Restaurant for lunch and she often struck up a conversation with Pam if they sat at one of her tables.

Then, at 3:00 p.m, she would pick up Laura at school.

The girls were glad their grandparents were coming for Thanksgiving, and had made interesting looking objects to bring home. Becky had made a round-bodied turkey on brown construction paper and glued rainbow colored feathers on it that stuck out in many directions. Laura had made a cornucopia basket out of woven strips of cardboard that could be put on the table as a centerpiece. Catherine taped the feathered turkey to the overhead pewter chandelier in the dining room, and placed the cornucopia on the old table. She didn't have a table cloth as long and narrow as that table was, but the pine wood seemed well finished, and she hoped nothing would make marks on it.

The night before Thanksgiving, she took down the dinner plates to prepare for the arrival of her parents. The next morning, while looking out the window, Laura exclaimed, "Mommy! Come and see! Maybe Daddy is coming, too!"

Catherine's heart jumped into her throat. She looked out the window to see her parents' car followed by other cars. As they pulled up and stopped, Laura and Becky ran outside onto the front porch. Catherine stood behind them and saw her brothers and sisters and their children all coming to be with her for Thanksgiving. She started to cry.

"I guess it's not Daddy," said Laura.

"Is that why you're crying, Mommy?" asked Becky.

"No, no honey, I am happy to see my sisters and brothers. I am just happy they all came."

Her parents enfolded Laura and Becky in their arms and guided everyone inside.

WINTER 1974-1975

...Dream on, dream on,
Dream yourself a dream come true
Dream on, dream on
Dream until your dream come true...

Steven Tyler, Aerosmith,
"Dream On," *Aerosmith,* 1973

Chapter 4

The sparkling white snow-covered road that led to the picturesque farmhouse looked absurdly clean.

The leafless maple trees poked through the rising banks of snow which trimmed their branches with white peaks. The back of the house was guarded by a group of old pines, and they, too, were frosted white. The snow blanketed the smooth, rising meadows on either side of the house and barn, creating an image of a chef-inspired cake. Even the black roof was white with snow, save for the area around the chimney. It was so deep in the driveway next to the barn that the cars had to park on the narrow plowed road, pressed into the sides of raised snow banks. Rarely traveled in the winter, the road had become narrower with every snowstorm. Candlelight twinkled warmly in the windows, branches of an enormous Christmas tree could be seen in the two-story adjoining room between house and barn, and music by a great new band, Aerosmith, seeped outside, floating away into the starry, moonlit night.

Catherine stood in front of the mirror in the entryway, and looked at all of her friends jostling each other. They were trying on the different hats and mittens she had somehow learned to knit since moving to the farm. Some of the stocking hats were striped and four or five feet long in bright, rainbow colors like drawings from a Dr. Seuss book. As they passed the hats around and laughed and joked, she felt almost happy. In preparation of wearing one of the hats, she gathered her long, blonde hair into an elastic band at the nape of her neck. Tonight, everyone who was at the old farm had either moved in and lived there, or was visiting so that she wouldn't be alone this first Christmas without Laura and Becky.

She had stayed on after the summer, contrary to Daniel's requests that she return to Boston. Attorney Farley had said she must never leave the state until it was safe to do so. He didn't want the divorce thrown into Massachusetts. Their summer home had become her real home, to become herself, but it was exacting a high price. She had taken a stand, hoping it wasn't like Custer's. Her wish to live in the country all year had come true—but not in the way she had hoped. Embroiled in the ongoing custody battle that had to be settled in order to divorce, it was wearing her thin on all levels: emotionally, physically and spiritually. Daniel used her decision to stay on the farm as a further example of her inappropriate and erratic behavior.

Catherine glanced at the framed newspaper clipping she had recently hung on the closet door where they were all gathering. Another reminder of last summer's arguments with Daniel about her political leanings and involvements being too far left, and his displeasure at her collection of posters from radical political groups. Before they had left for Vermont, he had grabbed all of her posters and torn them into a million pieces, but Catherine hid her cut out from *The Real Paper*[8]. She had been intrigued by the people selling the newspapers on Boylston Street by Boston Common.

They wore such interesting clothing and had long hair. And, they all used the "f" word. She didn't know at the time that her social mores and New England upbringing were beginning to shift. She questioned the old, tired, accepted ideas of marriage and family, and the views of her parents. Her framed article about how good sex is for you with a photograph showing a nude couple in the act of copulation was the first thing she hung up in their bedroom when they moved in for the summer.

"Is that the sort of thing our children should see hanging on the wall, when we have collected such fine, original oil paintings because of my professional connections?" Daniel had asked, late one night during another argument.

Catherine had replied, simply, "It's my connection, I like it. The Constitution gives us freedom of expression— what difference does it make if it's music, or art, or speech. Our society's views toward women are antiquated and they need to change—"

"Right, sure they do. Just what we need, more freedom for guys to look like girls with hair down to their asses, and girls burning bras to be femin-Nazis."

"Daniel, you know as well as I that women don't have the same rights men do—"

"Since when? Since you started reading all this crap and joining all these groups of wackos?"

Why don't I see it his way anymore? She had asked herself, backing down. *But, why can't women do the same things men do, like having sex with whomever they want? Why isn't sex part of our lives?*

Now, it hung in the entryway as a statement of her freedom. It was hard for her to remember when they seemed to agree on everything. It was hard for her to recall the sequence of events that had led to where she was now, going through such a contentious divorce and custody battle. The more she learned about women's history, for example, the more she recognized that treating women as if they were supposed to be a certain way or fulfill certain functions to complement men was wrong. Men became presidents of companies. Women became secretaries. Men became pilots of airlines. Women became stewardesses. The few women who stepped out of these roles were vilified, called lesbians or ugly women who no man would marry anyway. Her new housemates agreed that that was the sort of "societal bullshit from the ruling class of the great, white male." Eli and Davy were both quick to add, "Don't trust anyone over thirty."

After the separation, Catherine went to her bank to get a credit card in her name. It was denied—unless her husband would sign for her—even though she was co-owner of their home. It would take years of working before she would be granted the privilege.

She had been uncertain of herself, her future, and how she would manage everything on her own for the first time. The house seemed huge being there all alone.

Just after Thanksgiving, she received an unexpected phone call. Her close friend, Nina, had telephoned explaining that she and her husband had separated, too, and could she come to the farm to live with her two sons. Catherine told her to come, of course. "There's plenty of room and the kids can go to school together. It will be good for them." Nina was so pleased—she would arrive within days with a rented truck of furniture—driven by her new boyfriend, Davy.

While Catherine was thinking it would be a relief to have a friend to commiserate with, and that the children would have new playmates, Erin, six, the same age as Laura and Nathan, four—she hadn't known that Nina had a new boyfriend who would turn out to be a teenager.

As Catherine got the logistics of her new housemates worked out—Laura and Becky would be sharing a bedroom again—their schedules began to fit into place. Then, a friend of Davy's, named Eli, came to visit from the University of Connecticut. Then Eli's friend, Lenora came to visit—and that's when things began to get out of control.

Now, along with the ongoing custody battle, she was defending her right to live in what appeared to be a commune. Her new friends began calling her "Cat" rather than Catherine. Nina said it suited her. Since she had never had a nickname before, she felt a bit special.

And, her new friends had named the old farm, "Cat's Cradle," to define the place as a relaxing change from the busy, urban lives they had all been leading. Cat had been told by her friends that people in town began calling it "the Cradle Commune" once the house had filled up with Nina, Davy, Erin, Nathan, Eli, and Lenora. With the divorce proceedings that lay ahead, the last thing she wanted was to have the townspeople think her home was a commune.

Every evening after the children were put to bed, Nina, Davy, Eli and Lenora went into the family room and smoked marijuana. Cat had never smoked it before, but Nina thought she needed to try some for her nerves. One evening, after she checked to be sure the children were asleep, she went into the family room to try a little and see if it would be good for her.

"No," said Nina, "like this." Nina pursed her lips and took what appeared to be a sip of the joint and held her breath in. Then, she let it out. "See?"

"Okay, I'll try," said Cat.

At first, nothing happened, then she began having a tingly feeling that was both energizing and relaxing at the same time. Tingle, tingle, tingle—like a buzz. "Is that why they call it 'getting buzzed?'" she blurted out.

Everyone laughed and the laughter rippled softly. She felt a warm sensation coming from her friends that she hadn't noticed before. After her indoctrination into getting high, she understood why everyone should smoke marijuana. *Maybe it would bring about world peace.*

On this cold Christmas eve, Cat and her friends had raided her closet under the stairs to don her knitted creations, borrow extra jackets and boots, and prepare to brave the blustery, winter's night to drive the ten miles to church in the little village. Learning to knit and sew was part of her transformation from city life to country life. Her waist-length hair and penchant for wearing handmade prairie dresses separated Cat from her former life: wearing Newbury Street clothing, being photographed at all the formal events, and attending charitable balls. She enjoyed the change, thinking she had only traded one set of costumes for another. Before last summer's move to the farm, she had donated most of her clothes to charity and began buying used jeans with holes in them at the Lodge on Newbury Street. She began driving herself instead of having Daniel's chauffeur usher her around. It was a leap of faith driving in unfamiliar areas at first, but she had eventually managed. A few parking tickets, a few dissenting remarks from Daniel, but she had worked it out. It was much easier for her to drive in rural Vermont than in downtown Boston. She still got lost, but now she wasn't so afraid when she did that there would be one way streets and no turning back.

She relished the times when she could be absorbed in knitting again, but ever since her friends had moved in, there wasn't much quiet time to do so. It seemed like the old farm had taken on a new life where various people continued to show up uninvited, wanting to know more about what they were doing. Most asked questions were "Is this a real commune?" and, "Do you need more people living here?" Cat answered "No" on both accounts. Sometimes she would find herself defending her standoffishness to Nina, Davy and Eli. They wanted her to be more welcoming. Invite more people in.

"I'm not adding anyone else to this place," Cat said to Nina more than once. "It's already more than I can handle." Her attorney was less than pleased with this turn of events. They spoke regularly as the legal wheels slowly ground on over the holidays.

Cat felt responsible. Not only for her daughters and the custody lawsuit but after all, it was only half her home. She and Daniel jointly owned it. And, it was on the market and would have to be sold.

Her intention when they bought the farm was to have a real family room where she and her husband and their daughters could gather. The loft would be a guest room. The barn board closet would house the children's toys at the end of the day which would please Daniel as he hated messiness and toys everywhere. They would toast marshmallows in the new fireplace on cold winter nights while sipping hot cocoa. They would all sit together, and talk, and play board games. The long sofa with soft pillows and large, pine-plank coffee table was just the thing as it had a cabinet underneath that held games of all kinds. She had wistfully thought their unraveling marriage would re-knit itself and they would live in the country, happily ever after. She held that vision through all the problems with having the room completed. When the family room was close to being finished, the unforgiveable event of Daniel taking her daughters had splintered any thought of working things out. *A finished family room. A finished marriage.*

With everyone dressed up in the winter accessories, they looked like the cover of a colorful knitting book, albeit mixed more than matched. Cat thought everyone would enjoy singing Christmas carols at the festive midnight candlelight service, even though no one—other than Catherine—had ever been to such a service before. Cat looked forward to the ceremony of lighting candles and singing Christmas carols.

Jessica and Gene, who spent time at the commune before building their new log cabin, had arrived to drive with them. Cat first met them at the High Health Food Cooperative where she shopped. Jessica had been a groupie with a band where Gene had been a roadie. When they met, it was love at first sight. They married and moved to the country, building their log home themselves. They had many friends help out and had introduced Cat to Marty Zolov, a graduate student at Boston University. He was only a few years younger than Cat, not like Davy who was just out of high school.

Marty became Cat's first lover after her separation. He was looking forward to trying out the local church. Cat enjoyed him so much as he always seemed to be in such a good mood, and he helped offset her own feelings of living on a roller coaster that had gone out of control.

As they prepared to drive to the quaint New England church at the center of the small town, Eddie and Amy pulled up, passing joints to everyone for the ride. Davy and Eli knew them from their extended circle of friends in Cambridge who had gone to the University of Connecticut.

"Just in time!" said Eddie.

"You're not kidding!" replied Davy.

Cat wasn't sure about smoking pot and driving and Marty noticed her expression.

"Hey, it's okay to smoke and drive, honest. If anything, it will make us all drive more carefully!"

Cat smiled up at Marty. "Maybe just a few tokes."

Upon entering the church, Marty led the way to the front row of pews. When the service began, the special Christmas program was passed out. The group's spirited singing was exponentially enhanced by the joints they smoked while driving to town. Eddie and Amy had acquired a special Hawaiian-grown brand that was particularly heady. Not to be outdone, the entire congregation was moved to sing along with this exuberant group of newcomers. They seemed totally engaged in their singing.

Cat stood next to Marty. He was 6'6" and wore his curly, black hair in an Afro and sported a full beard. He had arrived from BU for his Christmas break to spend some time with her since it was her first Christmas without her children. Or, that's what he told her.

Next stood Nina. After moving to the farm and sending her two boys to school with Cat's two girls, she was having her first Christmas without her children as well. While her divorce-in-process was much less antagonistic than Cat's, but the court stipulated that her sons would spend all holidays with their father, which upset Nina terribly. She could barely imagine what Cat was going through in her custody battle when she could still have most of the time with her boys.

Nina had let her hair grow really long and it looked similar to Davy's. Sometimes, they would both wear their hair in one, long braid. They were the same height, and from the back, you could barely tell them apart. Nina enjoyed that immensely.

Holding Nina's hand, Davy stood by her side. He was an angelic-looking man of 18, and he was very supportive and consoling to Nina in her divorce woes. The boys really liked him, too. He had been their babysitter for years.

When Nina had decided to move out of her home and take the boys away to Vermont, Davy had asked to go too, revealing his love for Nina. She was surprised, but was very drawn to him physically and wanted to enjoy this new experience.

Now, Davy worked in the village at the restaurant part of the time to defray his expenses. He still wanted to continue his education at some point, and he was putting together a portfolio. He eventually wanted to go to the Orson Welles Film School[9] in Cambridge. Nina supported this endeavor; after all, he was a good decade younger than her. She didn't have any illusions about their relationship being long-term. She just wanted to have some fun.

Next stood Eli, Davy's friend, who had graduated from the same high school a few years ahead of him, and had decided to visit the commune after hearing Davy talk about it. As a student at the University of Connecticut, Eli began visiting weekends. Romanticizing the country life of a small village in Vermont that boasted a summer theater known as the Grande Blanc, Eli took a leave of absence from college that would turn into an entire semester. He became the nanny for the children when Nina and Cat began to work at their jobs.

A 6'4" black man who wore one dangly gold earring, Eli's presence was unusual in what was considered the whitest state in the country. Most everyone on the commune wore blue jeans, t-shirts and work shirts, while Eli chose togas and exotic fabrics that looked hand woven. He liked clothes that had a theatrical flair to them, a little bit of movement. Eli's best friend, Lenora, often referred to him as a "drama queen," which Eli loved, as he hoped somehow to get into the summer theater group. But people often thought, in Eli's case, that he *was* the summer theater, and had arrived early to prepare for the season.

Cat wondered what Daniel's reaction would be had he known that Eli was—for all intents and purposes—the replacement for Anna, the British nanny they had had in Boston.

Next to Eli stood Lenora. She and Eli met at a Gay Liberation gathering at UConn. She had been living at an alternative farm and commune in Connecticut to support being a student. Part of the bylaws of living on that farm and growing organic produce was a 30 hour-a-week work commitment. Exhausted, she dropped out of school and had simply followed Eli to Vermont.

Lenora needed some time in the country while she got her head together. She was a chunky, freckled redhead, and she and Eli were happy to appear as a stunning couple. Her rather pinkish skin-tone and light brown hair contrasted beautifully with Eli's rich, brown coloring. They were proud of their homosexuality at a time when it was just beginning to come to the attention of the mainstream--and not very well received.

Next to Lenora stood Eddie and Amy. Having arrived in time for the Christmas festivities, they thought of themselves as occasional residents—their drug business in New England and New York City kept them too busy to spend much time in one place. Eddie had dark brown, shoulder-length curly hair, a trim beard, was quite short and thin, and laughed all the time. Amy had wild, long black hair and appeared elf-like in her stature and naive, sweet facial expressions. They were the most soft-spoken of the group. It was hard for anyone to believe that they were two of the most successful drug dealers on the eastern seaboard, spending a good deal of their time staying one step ahead of the law. When they were at the farm, they made it their mission to roll joints, fill pipes and make sure everyone was sufficiently stoned. Nina had been buying marijuana from them since Davy's friend Eli introduced them to her. They had all become friends when Nina was still living in Boston. Nina didn't really know how much drug dealing Eddie and Amy did, but she found it all amusing.

And, next to Eddy and Amy were Cat's friends from the High Health Food Cooperative, Jessica and Gene. Recently, they had both cut their long hair due to having to get real jobs so that they could finish building their log home. Jessica's shoulder-length soft, brown hair now blended in with the townspeople in appearance, and Gene's short haircut made him look as straight as an arrow. They lived just a town away, were still working on details of the interior, and had stored some of their things in Cat's barn. They enjoyed visiting the commune and often dropped in when Eddie and Amy arrived with a new supply of hashish or marijuana. Eddie and Amy's visit was always a reason for getting together, sharing a meal, playing music and getting high. Gene's experience with the band had gotten him interested in playing guitar, and Jessica played the tambourine, reminders of their traveling days. Lenora, surprisingly, played a flute delicately which often wasn't heard over the rest of the music. The kids were impressed. Davy had bongos (though he would have liked a complete set of drums). Cat wondered how she could handle a set of drums in the family room if that happened. Eli liked to sing. Nina and Eli would sometimes sing together. Cat wished she could play an instrument, find something she was good at doing besides knitting.

Jessica and Gene planned to return to the commune to party afterwards.

Most of the people in the church had been living in the town for generations. Cat wondered what the townspeople thought of her and everyone living at the farm, or if they now thought it was a commune. And, if the Christmas Eve service was very different tonight because of their presence.

Marty sang the loudest of them all, and knew every word of every Christmas carol, which Cat thought was pretty good since he was Jewish. This was the sort of church-going holiday ceremony she had enjoyed all of her life, but she had never had one with friends quite like these.

She wore her holiday prairie dress of red, yellow and blue calico print fabric that she had made to match her daughters'. Cat looked over at her friend Nina, who seemed as engrossed with singing as everyone. Cat's thoughts drifted to her children, to the events of the separation that had led up to what she was presently going through.

As long-time friends, this coincidental timing of their separations was still a surprise for Cat. For one thing, Nina had never mentioned any marital discontent to her. It seemed like Cat was the one with the complaints in the past few years whenever they got together. They were both influenced by the political unrest of the late 60's, and by the conversations with their friends who had returned from the Vietnam War. Even though their involvement in antiwar demonstrations had brought them closer together, Cat realized between Nina's telephone call and subsequent arrival with her teenage boyfriend, she hadn't seen it coming at all.

Back at the church, Marty flashed a smile at her. He had such perfect teeth, a dazzling smile and dark, mischievous eyes. She found herself pulled back into the moment, singing Christmas carols with everyone else.

After the singing, the minister led them in a prayer for peace, turned off the electric lights, and small candles set in little paper drip-catchers were lit, passing the flame from one to another, row by row. At the end of the service when the lights came back on so that the congregation could see to file out, lines formed at the end of each pew to follow the minister to the door. As they took their turn walking past the minister, he grasped each of their hands in a firm handshake and grinned ear-to-ear. "Thank you for coming," he repeated over and over. And, "Please come back to our regular services."

They received many thanks and appreciative comments from the delighted townspeople who enjoyed their energy and enthusiasm.

They were surprised to be so openly welcomed since they all felt like outsiders. Whenever they went into town, they were always being asked in the stores and at the gas station if they lived "on that commune." After all, they were the only hippies in town.

As Cat's friends piled into their cars, they were still smiling widely, still high from the joints they had smoked on the ten-mile trip into town. Driving home first was Nina with Davy at the wheel of her Datsun. He liked the car to slip and slide on the smooth, snowy roads. While Cat knew he was still growing up, she lacked the patience for his youthful behavior. She watched the car hoping he wouldn't drive too fast particularly in winter weather. Eli and Lenora rode with them.

Cat was glad that she and Marty had taken her Jeep, and she had adjusted the settings on the hubs of the wheels into four-wheel-drive before leaving the commune, just to be safe. Eddie and Amy rode in the back. Jessica and Gene followed in their pickup truck. When Cat, Marty, Eddie and Amy arrived home, Davy greeted them at the door as if he had been there for hours, instead of only minutes before they arrived.

"Hot cocoa and brownies?" he asked, holding a plate of delicious-smelling warm brownies under their noses.

"Yes, perfect!" Marty replied, eyes bright.

Everyone converged in the kitchen where Nina was already making a pot of hot cocoa. Eli was checking the rest of the brownies he had left in the oven before they went to church so they would still be warm when they returned.

"Hmmmmm," Eli said, tearing off a corner of one brownie. "It's the hashish that makes them so good!"

As they sat around the kitchen table and talked about the enjoyable evening, Cat almost didn't miss her daughters, at least for the moment.

"Weren't you surprised as to how nice everyone was to us?" asked Lenora.

"I sure was," said Eli.

"Yeah, I guess it was pretty amazing," said Eddie as he expertly rolled a joint with one hand.

"I love singing Christmas carols!" said Marty.

"How did you learn them?" asked Cat.

"Oh, I grew up with a friend who always had me to his home for Christmas Eve since my family didn't celebrate it. His mom played the piano and we all sang together. I think my parents knew but they never said anything about it."

Nina and Davy came into the kitchen." We have a surprise in the family room—everyone bring blankets."

Everyone went to their respective bedrooms for blankets and then went into the family room and climbed the ladder to the loft.

"It's a love-in!" Davy and Nina yelled out. "A love-in!"

Lenora laughed, "Oh goodie, all these male and female couples, now who do I get to be with?"

Votive candles were lit around the loft banisters and everyone began taking off their clothes. Cat's eyes opened wide as she stood there at the top of the ladder. Davy, Nina and Lenora lay down in the center of the pile of blankets and pillows, and began kissing each other. Eli, Eddie and Amy joined them as Jessica and Marty snuggled in to one side. Gene held his hand up and gestured to Catherine, "Come on Cat, the water's fine," he joked.

"I – I," Cat began.

Marty stood up, walked over to her and brought her into the group.

"I'll take care of you, Cat, don't worry."

Eventually, sated by the events of the evening and the hash-laced brownies, they all slept together like a litter of puppies.

For awhile, Catherine wasn't able to think about the turmoil and fears of losing her daughters. In fact, she couldn't think at all.

Well so, so long, my honey, so long.

Too bad you had to drift away

'Cause I could use some company

Right here on this road, on this road today

Janis Joplin, lyrics

"Bye-Bye Baby," *Joplin In Concert (Live),* 1972

Chapter 5

Just days before New Year's, nothing was quite taking shape. Marty said he had "prior commitments," and Cat was angry and upset with him. She wondered if there was someone else he would rather be with. Cat had wanted everything to be casual in their relationship and keep it open-ended; no commitment. She wanted to be cool like all the other people she was meeting. But, she had also wanted him to be there for her New Year's Eve gathering, and now he was leaving.

Davy's mother kept calling, asking him to come home. He said she was mad that he didn't come home for Christmas. After several calls in a row, Nina snatched the phone out of Davy's hand to talk to her directly. Cat came into the kitchen in time to watch Nina's expression go from simple aggravation to shocked surprise. She hung up and stared at Davy.

"Davy—is it true? Are you only 17-years-old? Your mother just wants you to finish high school?" Nina asked, her face pale. "How could you lie to me about your age, Davy?"

"It's not that far off, Nina, I'll be eighteen--"

"Just leave! I want you to leave!" Nina yelled and stormed upstairs.

Davy turned toward Cat with his big, innocent eyes.

"Cat, listen, I love Nina!"

"You can't lie about your age, Davy, you could jeopardize her having custody of her children. You must know that."

"But, but—I didn't think it was that big a deal."

"Well, it is. My God, Davy! Nina could go to jail for having sex with a minor! You better go home and finish high school anyway—take the bus to Boston with Marty since he isn't staying for New Years'."

"But—but—"

"No buts. Get your bags packed. You're leaving."

Lucky me, thought Cat, as she drove Marty and Davy to the bus stop in the nearest town—a good 35 miles away.

She hadn't been back since taking Daniel that long ago summer's day. It was at least an hour's drive in the winter and you could cut the silence with a knife. Cat didn't feel like talking to Marty or Davy. The entire trip was quiet, save for the music on the only radio station they would come in. As he got out of the Jeep, Davy said he'd be back. He got out and walked around to the back for his baggage. Marty turned toward her while she stared straight ahead, and gave her a pleading look.

"Didn't I stay with you for Christmas? Didn't I?"

When she didn't respond, he turned and slowly stepped out of the Jeep with his rucksack. As soon as he closed the door, Cat didn't plan to wait and see the bus come. Gritting her teeth, she drove off too fast and spun the rear tires, spraying them both with snow and sand from the road.

Assholes, Cat said to herself.

In her rearview mirror, she could see them standing there with hangdog looks on their faces, watching her drive away.

Cat wondered if she would ever be able to be as laidback the way everyone else seemed to be about open relationships and casual sex. She knew when she got her daughters back after vacation from Daniel that she wouldn't want to have them see her smoking pot. Or living with a younger man, or with any man. Nor was she ready to explain about homosexuals. Nina felt fine about smoking pot in front of the kids, but Cat didn't. Nina and Lenora criticized her for being too uptight.

Cat, Nina, Eli and Lenora were still talking over what to do for New Year's Eve after a wonderful fresh pasta supper Eli had prepared. They passed a joint around and thought perhaps a few phone calls to nearby friends might find something going on.

They called Jessica and Gene, who were always working on their log cabin.

"We were just talking about you guys and New Years' Eve, but," Jessica said, "I don't want to be buggered by Davy again. After the Christmas Eve love-in, I could barely walk."

Cat told her the news—that Davy was 17 and had gone home to his mother. Jessica was horrified. "Omigod! Jail bait!"

"No, no, everything's fine," Cat said. "He'll be 18 in a month or so and he wants to be with Nina after he finishes high school."

As the planning for a New Years' Eve party gained momentum, Jessica called some other friends, Pam and Brad, who worked at Whitey's Restaurant. It was the only one in town where most people went. Otherwise, you had to drive miles to the next town for a restaurant that served dinners and drinks. Pam and Brad were always up for a good time, well, Pam was. She had spoken with Catherine often at Whitey's the days she stopped by to have lunch with Becky before picking up Laura at school.

When Cat and Daniel had first moved to the farm house last summer, they had eaten there quite regularly while getting their renovations done. Later, Pam had heard all the rumors of the separation, pretty much like everyone in the small town had.

Eli was preparing little bowls of ice cream for dessert when he pulled out a business card from the kitchen drawer. He had met an interesting woman at the local High Health Food Cooperative and thought they should call her.

"When I was shopping for the babies," as he affectionately called the children, "we were chatting about preparing soybeans. She has long, white hair, and wears lots of velvet and crystals." He handed the card to Cat.

Eli had asked the interesting looking woman whatever she was doing living in the middle of nowhere. He found out she had moved to Vermont from Greenwich Village several years ago and was trying to make a living working at the health food store and doing her esoteric work. She had given him her card which was bright purple with pale, pink letters. The card read, "Ceremonies and Chakra

Clearings by Lavender Mountaincloud." A phone number was listed, Cat called the number, and it was answered almost immediately.

"Lavender speaking."

"Hello, Lavender," Cat started, "I'm Cat at the Cradle Commune. Eli said he met you at the High Health Food Cooperative." Cat paused to see if Lavender remembered.

"Oh, right, yes, I remember."

"Great, great, I was wondering if you were available for New Year's Eve for a couple of hours for a ceremony of some kind, Eli mentioned chakra clearing? I know it's a bit last minute...."

"New Year's Eve is fine; it will be just after the full moon this year so we should be all right. Mercury isn't in retrograde till the end of January." She was also thinking that she hadn't made any money for over a month and this couldn't have come at a better time.

"What? Well, I am really glad you are available."

"Not a problem, but now I must leave for a ceremony I am doing at the library. Chakra clearing is a great way to begin the New Year."

"Sounds good," said Cat, who then found out the cost, and asked what time to expect her to arrive.

"I should be there around 8:30 or 9:00 p.m. but, all ceremony needs to be completed before the New Year begins. I like to be home by then."

"Fine, fine," Cat said, and hung up, a bit mystified by the whole conversation. She had never heard of chakra clearings but she seemed to have just asked for one. Nor had she heard of Mercury in retrograde, or anything else this woman named Lavender alluded to.

They all discussed how to divide up the cost, called back Jessica and Pam to get their agreement, and the plans were set.

Everyone was very excited about clearing their charkas once they found out what they were—energy centers along the length of the spine and body. Scott, a cousin of Gene's was planning to come up during that week too, so of course he would be invited to the event. Gene also mentioned inviting Cheryl and Sam, who usually lived in a tepee but were staying at a winter rental a few towns away. Cat had heard Jessica and Gene talk about Cheryl and Sam before but hadn't met them yet as they never had a telephone for ease of contact. Spring, summer and fall, they lived on some land of Sam's family that was way out in the middle of nowhere and winters they would find a rental for the coldest months. Cheryl and Sam were devotees of the cause for Native Americans. Sam felt a kinship with the traditional ways he had learned from his years of study and participation in many powwows. His interest began long before he went to Vietnam, but after Vietnam, he had made a tepee and lived in it as part of his recovery from the experience that had so negatively affected him. Cat had been forewarned not to bring it up, that Sam didn't want to discuss it. He had spent years living with several Native American tribes out west and attending peyote ceremonies to heal his emotional wounds. She was curious about Sam—and Cheryl, too.

Cat was fine about having more people come to the party.

Since they didn't have a telephone, it was agreed that whoever was headed in their direction would stop by to invite them in the next day or two. In the end, Gene had to go to a supply store fairly close to Sam and Cheryl. He always needed some part or other for their log cabin so he volunteered.

Between 8:00-8:30 p.m. on New Year's Eve, the invited guests showed up bringing wine, joints, food and desserts for later. The lights weren't on in the front of the house so people naturally went to the middle door of the family room where the Christmas tree lights were always on.

As they all filed directly into the family room, Cat said to Nina they had better start a fire in the fireplace. It wasn't very warm yet but the fire wouldn't take along to make it comfortable. There were pegs along the wall which made it easy for hanging winter coats up, and the seating would be enough for all the visitors. The door was open in the hallway to the kitchen where Eli directed the depositing of food.

"Right this way for your dishes, right on the kitchen table," he offered. "Oh, what is that? That looks interesting!" Always the main chef and grocery shopper, Eli had to check what everyone brought. "Did you make that yourself? No? Oh." He sniffed, disappointed to those who brought something bought from a store. He admired Cheryl's polenta that she had made herself, from scratch, and he asked for the recipe.

No one knew or really understood anything about chakra clearing[10], except for Scott, Gene's cousin. He lived in Cambridge, knew all about chakras, so that had been part of the discussion before Lavender arrived.

"She'll probably begin with the root chakra, at the base of the spine, where your sexual energy flows from," Scott had said. The women all listened intently. "You need to raise the energy upward. In Tantric sex, you focus the energy in order to keep your erection for an hour or more before coming."

"Ohhh," several women said together. Gene raised his eyebrows and nodded at Sam, who winked. Gene rolled his eyes.

At a little after 9:00 p.m. Lavender Mountaincloud pulled up in her old purple Volvo, parked in front of the house, and walked in through the front door. Cat came out from the kitchen to greet her and take her purple coat.

"I'll keep it with me, thanks anyway," Lavender said.

She brought Lavender into the family room that was lit primarily with candles.

"This is lovely," Lavender announced, "and if we could move the sofas back and the tables, and sit on the rug in a circle, even better."

The eager participants were milling around, waiting for whatever was about to happen. "Sure, let's do it," chorused the group who quickly responded and got to work. Hearing about chakra clearings was so new; it had piqued everyone's interest. They were all too happy to oblige this eccentric-looking woman dressed in purple velvet robes and crystal earrings. Her long, flowing white hair moved with her as she turned her head to observe the seating arrangement.

The sofas were moved, pillows and throws were put on the floor in a circle and all gathered to sit down, curious about the coming event.

Lavender's hair settled around her as she sat in a cross-legged position on a pillow she carried in with her. Her velvet skirt and top were edged with small beads and she carried a velvet sack with shiny beads trimming the handle. From it she drew a group of various-sized bells, which she positioned in front of her knees. She invited everyone to go to center, breathe deeply, and to "bring their consciousness into a meditative state." Everyone willingly complied, except for Pam who kept one eye open to watch Lavender.

Catherine's thoughts strayed to her two daughters and she wondered what they were doing at their father's home as she tried to breathe deeply while sitting in a cross-legged position. Nina wondered what Davy was doing at his mother's house and if she would see him again. Lenora was thinking about the white-haired, interesting woman, and wondered if she was a lesbian, too. Eli missed Davy, he was so cute, and sometimes Eli and he would go off to be alone and fool around together. Eli thought Davy was really gay. Davy secretly thought he might be bisexual and while he would let Eli fondle him, he didn't let it go too far. Gene's cousin, Scott, was as tall and dark as Gene was—and very good-looking. He had an easy smile that seemed to hold a secret. All the women noticed him, except Lenora.

Jessica and Gene had just had sex with a neighbor before they arrived which Jessica had found mildly disturbing seeing Gene make out with another man. But then they had both given her their undivided attention and she was very, very relaxed. Fortunately, Scott arrived after they had gotten out of the shower or Jessica supposed he would have wanted to be part of it, too. She always thought everyone wanted her. Having traveled with a rather well-known band, Jessica found it hard to ever really be content without the excitement of new sex partners and drugs being present. Gene didn't mind since the idea of fidelity wasn't one he had ever entertained. His roadie days that became a total burn out weren't very far behind him.

Cheryl and Sam were hoping there would be coals left to start a fire with when they returned to their barely-insulated, drafty winter home. Cat had offered them the loft for the night. It was cold without the fire in the fireplace, but Cat had said, "I can just turn on the electric heat! No big deal!"

Cheryl and Sam had talked about Cat having an electrically heated farmhouse.

"She must have a lot of money to be able to do that," Cheryl had said.

"Or, like she told us," Sam answered, "it was to be for summers only and she didn't know she would be staying through the winter months. Besides, it's already been listed on the market. Some flatlander will probably buy it—then those other parties we have heard about will be over." Sam smiled ruefully. He was glad they had come to this gathering in the bitter cold winter. Getting together with friends, and the ease of hanging out in a house that was warm, felt wonderful.

Pam and Brad hadn't had sex in months, and Pam was wondering about Scott as a possibility to get her needs met. At this point, she felt like she could do every man in the room.

Lavender's rising voice returned everyone to the moment as she began chanting about the sky and earth, and shaking a little gourd rattle. She began to sing in another language, then breathed in and out deeply and made a whooshing sound. It sounded sexual and Cat opened one eye. The group began to stir.

Then, Lavender shifted into a slow, long, ommmmmmm sound and invited everyone to make the sound with her as they breathed in and out. When it ended, she asked everyone to hold hands in the circle.

They all moved in more closely to join hands. She asked them to call in their spirit guides, which few knew about, and didn't really know what to do. Noticing their quizzical expressions, Lavender led them first through a spirit guide ritual to assist them. *What planet are these people living on?* Lavender thought to herself. She wondered how people today could avoid learning this information these days. She was going to have to require that people understood some of this or start giving pre-ceremony classes. At the library, she often gave talks there to drum up business for her readings and chakra clearings.

Then, satisfied that they were all moving along together, she began to chant for the spirit guides to attend this meeting of kindred souls and, suddenly, all the lights went out. There were enough lit candles, and they often lost electricity in the winter, so Cat wasn't particularly concerned. Everyone was looking around in the candlelit room to get their bearings.

"Perhaps there is more dark energy here than I first noticed," Lavender said, taking loss of electricity as having a deeper meaning. "Let's clear our chakras of any blockages that could prevent energy from flowing freely." Then, she began the clearing instructions in a mesmerizing voice with a lulling cadence.

"The chakras are like a string of pearls, one following the other from the base of the feet, through the top of the head and outward—up, up into the universe. We will focus on the seven main chakras beginning at the base of the spine, the seat of the Kundalini. Once we open the Kundalini[11], the goddess Shakti awakens, uncoils and rises upward clearing each chakra as she goes. The first chakra is red and we will begin by focusing on the color red. Now, spin the chakra clockwise, see it in your mind, like the hands of a clock, move it forward."

Everyone appeared to be concentrating on the visualization and following her directions as she scanned the room. All eyes were closed.

Lavender spoke slowly and deliberately, moving them through each chakra, one by one, and tinkling little bells as she introduced each color. Red, orange, yellow, green, blue, violet and finally a "soft-pinkish white."

Cat felt warm and happy, Nina was full of energy to the point of wanting to get up and dance, but she controlled herself. Eli experienced a truly peaceful feeling of warm affection toward all around him, and everyone seemed to be experiencing much the same. Except Pam. Pam wanted to screw every guy in the room and wondered how long she could take the exercise before tearing her clothes off.

After they reached the top of the head chakra, Lavender said that now Shakti would meet with Lord Shiva, the Supreme Being and in uniting, achieve a state of bliss.

"As we move our collective energy upward into the universe, please stand."

Everyone slowly pulled themselves to standing, feeling a bit off-balance.

"Now, we join hands and move close together in a warm, group hug."

The sensuality of the moment was like being inside a haze of liquid honey. Lavender brought them all back to reality with a bit about how "we are all one, and now we are all separate—release each other and move away from the circle."

From the grins on everyone's faces, and lumps in all the guys' jeans, most seemed to have had a genuinely moving experience. Not Pam. She was outraged that this woman had given her husband a hard-on, which she hadn't been able to do in months. With that, the lights came on, catching her expression in mid-glare.

Lavender rose to go and everyone hugged her and thanked her.

After Lavender left, Brad said to Pam, "Wow, that was amazing—"

Pam was headed into the front room for her coat, "Shut up, Brad, let's go." She didn't think she wanted to spend time at the commune anymore. She would see them in town, anyway, and they often visited Jessica and Gene. She didn't need this aggravation.

Jessica and Gene had brought a new album by Led Zeppelin and Nina put the record on Cat's small stereo system. Pam and Brad quickly left through the front door while everyone else began to dance.

I shot the sheriff
But I didnt shoot no deputy, oh no!
I shot the sheriff
But I didn't shoot no deputy, ooh, ooh, oo-ooh...

Bob Marley,
"I Shot The Sheriff," *Burnin'*, 1973

Chapter 6

In February, there was an ice storm to end all ice storms and the main news on the radio was all about the driving conditions. It was nearly 6:00 p.m. when Cat turned it on for an update.

"Interstate 89 has become a skating rink," the announcer began. "The combination of sleet and rain has frozen over the highway making driving treacherous and there's no end in sight."

"Geez, Lenora, Eli, did you hear that?" Cat asked.

"They must be on their way," Eli said. "Nina left early this morning. She was probably on the road by this afternoon."

"Maybe," said Lenora, "but that means she'll be driving right into the storm."

"Well, we'll give them awhile longer," said Cat.

"Then what?" asked Lenora.

"Then I'll call the police station and see if they have a highway patrol who may have heard something."

"Oh, that will be useful, particularly with them all smoking pot in the car."

"Nina wouldn't smoke pot in the car!"

"Right, Cat, sure, never happen. Like, we didn't smoke a doobie driving to church Christmas Eve." Lenora shook her head and walked away.

"I mean not while driving in a blizzard!"

Nina had driven to Boston early in the morning to drop off all four of the children at their respective fathers' for February vacation week. Then, she was going to drive to Cambridge to pick up Davy.

Davy had completed his unfinished senior year in high school by taking a GED program, and his mother had agreed to send him to the Orson Wells Film School in Cambridge. In February, he turned 18. His mother was pleased that he wasn't living at that hippie place in Vermont again.

Davy wanted to study filmmaking ever since he could remember and it had all worked out. Although he had missed New Year's Eve at the commune, Gene's cousin

Scott lived in a communal house full of students on Huron Avenue in Cambridge. When Nina found out, she put Davy in touch with Scott. More roommates meant less rent, so Scott was glad to have Davy join the household. Davy was able to move in mid-February and begin his new life. He still wanted to come up weekends as much as possible, and it was clear that Nina missed him.

Eddie and Amy had scored some super marijuana that they would bring up—if they could all fit in the car with the new stereo system Davy had gotten for Christmas. They didn't mention that they had had to leave their car at Boston Logan Airport and purchase new identities. After a recent deal in New York, when they were on the bus to their parking lot, a bunch of black cars were parked together surrounding their car. They told the bus driver that they had made a mistake about which parking lot and needed to get off at another one.

Davy wanted to bring his stereo to the commune where he could enjoy it weekends. The old one of Cat's wasn't very good and Davy knew that the new speakers would blast the music for miles.

Nina had managed to get one speaker in the trunk and the other lay across the backseat at an angle so that Amy and Eddie had to sit holding it on their laps. While they managed to get the other components into the trunk, no one could bring anything else with them. A few backpacks were stuffed on the floor around their legs, but that was all there was room for with the size of the new equipment. Davy put one of the components under his feet and held another in his lap.

Cat had made a pot of vegetarian stew per Lenora's request, but wondered why she did. *She could have picked out the meat,* she thought. *Why make such a big deal out of it?* Lenora was a bit of a thorn in her side; she was critical of everyone whether it was about gender issues, politics, or specifically, Cat's child raising. *Like, she has had children and is doing some great job raising them.*

Lenora was macramé-ing a plant hanger and Eli had started the fire in the fireplace in the family room. He was sad that the "babies" as he referred to his four charges, had gone away for the week. All in all, having Eli help out with Nina and Cat's work schedules had been very good.

Cat got a job at the only clothing store in town and Nina waitressed at Whitey's—something she had done in college. There weren't any interior design possibilities for Cat anywhere near where she lived, but she knew she should get out and work at something.

Eli was attentive to the children and an excellent cook, coming up with all sorts of ideas with the food that they had, which was primarily vegetarian. He wanted to be sure the children got enough protein, and consulted many cookbooks and talked to the women at the health food store for cooking tips. They just adored Eli. For some of them, he was the first homosexual they had ever met. For probably just as many, the very first black person ever. Some of them asked him for advice about their children. Eli always had a way of speaking to children that made them perk up. The men who worked at the health food store would glance at each other when the women were twittering about Eli. They were either jealous or annoyed by him, and most kept their distance.

Lenora, Eli and Cat had eaten the stew—and it wasn't half-bad with Eli's famous crab cakes on the side. The crabmeat was canned, but he made it very tasty with one of his many gourmet recipes. Cat always complimented him on his various food creations as she appreciated not having to cook very often.

Cat turned on the radio again as it drew closer to 8:00 p.m.

"We have received word from the Vermont State Police to not drive on the Interstate unless you are sanding it or you are in an emergency vehicle," the announcer said. "It is extremely dangerous and there are problems with tow trucks pulling cars out of the ditches. Some of the trucks attempting to pull out cars have slid over the embankments themselves."

Now, Cat was worried with the number of people in Nina's Datsun flying up the highway. Perhaps they had stayed in Cambridge—but, no, they would have called. *What if Nina had let Davy drive?* Cat decided to call the sheriff's office. There were two part-time policemen. One was the sheriff, and one was the deputy. She would ask if they had a highway patrol or if she would have to call the state police. She dialed the operator and asked to be connected to the police station.

"Deputy Shepherd," he answered on the first ring.

"Deputy Shepherd, this is Catherine Janson at the Sheldon farm," she said, remembering to use the name of the former owners, "and I have some housemates returning from Cambridge. I think that they left hours ago, and I am afraid they are stuck somewhere on Interstate 89."

"Well, I have a Land Rover and chains, I can get up on the highway and see if there are any cars in the past couple of exits, but that will take a good hour or so. What kind of car is it?"

"Oh! It's a red Datsun, a little car with four doors, and that would be wonderful if you could check on it. I would really appreciate it."

"No problem, m'am." Deputy Shepherd hung up the phone, shaking his head and muttering, "Bunch of no-account hippies, living in sin at the old Sheldon farmstead. Well, if I can't find any of 'em on the highway, I'll swing by there and take a look at the old farm myself."

At 10:30 p.m., Catherine looked out the front room window for the hundredth time; Lenora and Eli shared a joint by the fire. It was becoming eerie in the creaking farmhouse, and ice clacked against the windows from the frozen branches of the bushes and trees. The wind picked up, sounding like an old animal howling deep in the woods.

The radio buzzed on, turned low. Since they had taken the television to the dump last fall as a protest for the establishment poisoning their children's minds, there were few distractions from their natural surroundings—unless they were playing the latest rock 'n' roll music.

"Put on the Rolling Stones album, will you?" Cat called into Lenora and Eli.

As she turned away from the window, she thought she caught a glimpse of light coming up over the hill. She turned back, and sure enough, lights were flickering off the icy trees. She opened the front door and stepped onto the porch. She could hear the whirr of an engine as it made the crest of the hill and hoped it was Nina, and that the deputy had found them.

As the car came into view, it was the deputy's Land Rover. She saw smiling faces and hands waving as they pulled up in front of the farm house.

Cat grabbed the bucket of ashes on the porch and sprinkled them on the walk as she made her way to the Land Rover, relief washing over her.

"We made it! We thought we were going to spend the night in the car on the side of the highway!" Davy called out as he alighted from the Land Rover.

Catherine remembered the marijuana they were bringing up. *They must have left it in the car,* she thought.

"I'm so glad you are all safe! I kept getting these reports on the radio and I didn't know where you were!"

Nina jumped out of the back seat and hugged her. "We could have been in the car all night except for our knight in shining armor!" Nina pointed toward Deputy Shepherd.

The deputy assisted with the stereo components and speakers, and soon all the boxes from the back of the Land Rover were on the floor in the front room.

Cat hadn't thought about Eli and Lenora having a joint, but they had realized what was happening when she had gone outside and had closed the door to the family room. The lyrics of the song, Rolling Stones' song, "I Can't Get No Satisfaction" could be heard in the background.

She thanked Deputy Shepherd, as did everyone in turn. They were so grateful to be rescued. Being at odds with herself from anxiously waiting to find out if everyone was all right, she had made a pot of coffee to fill the time. "Would you like a cup of coffee? I just brewed it fresh."

"Sure, that'd be great before going back out," he replied. The Rolling Stones album continued playing but Cat noticed it had been turned down.

She went to the stove for the coffee pot and reached up for a mug. A small hashish pipe rolled out of the cupboard and she caught it with one hand and slipped it into her jeans pocket in one swift motion.

"What do you like in your coffee?"

"Black is fine."

"Please, sit down." Nina was grinning as she pulled out the chair at the kitchen table for the deputy. Then she and Davy sat at the kitchen table and told all about the adventure of sliding off the highway into a gully hours before. When they saw the Land Rover pull up on the highway, they didn't know if he could see their car over the embankment.

"We knew the black ice was treacherous and wondered if he was going to come sliding into us! But, he just slowed down and found us! We were so glad he could see our car!" said Nina.

"Then, he made his way on foot down the slope. We figured we should just leave the car till tomorrow, but

Deputy Shepherd helped us carry my new stereo up the embankment," added Davy.

As they told the story, Deputy Shepherd began to smile, too. He recognized their appreciation was genuine and that he was sitting in a well-kept kitchen, no dishes in the sink, no messiness, even the floors were clean. The things that had been said about the commune didn't look to be true. No one seemed to be on drugs, just very happy at being rescued. Very, very happy.

He wasn't much older than any of them, and he wondered what his life would be like if had wound up on a hippie commune instead of marrying Sue Ellen at eighteen years of age because he had gotten her pregnant. Everyone in town said that the people living at the old farm had no morals and would have sex with anyone. He wondered about that, too, since he thought Catherine was pretty good-looking.

"More coffee?" asked Cat.

"No, thanks." Smiling, Deputy Shepherd rose to leave. "I should check out a few more roads around town before I call it a night. Those little foreign cars don't do so well up here."

"Well, that's probably true," said Cat, thinking of how glad she was to have the Jeep.

"Thank you!" Everyone said in unison, and Cat thought Nina and Davy seemed a little too bright about it. Eddie and Amy were still unpacking stereo components in the front room. Cat walked Deputy Shepherd to the door and they stepped around the boxes on the way. "Careful on the ice," Cat said as she watched him go down the steps.

He gave a wave to her as he got into his Land Rover. She waved back and closed the door. She locked it, for once.

As she turned back toward the front room, Eddie looked up from one of the boxes he had opened.

"Nothing like getting a little help from the local deputy to carry in your weed!" Eddie said.

Davy hooted. "I guess we're lucky he didn't have a dope-sniffing dog!"

One of the boxes was opened for Cat to see, and packed around a stereo receiver were dozens of neatly rolled plastic bags of marijuana.

SPRING 1975

...I guess my feet know where they want me to go
Walking on a country road...

James Taylor
"Country Road," *Sweet Baby James*, 1970

Chapter 7

It was March, the first calendar day of spring, with snow on the ground. The night before, everyone at the commune had put on boots and coats to go outside, even though the moon was far from full, to welcome in the new season. The snow was too deep; they had to stay on the porch.

Eli had waxed eloquent about the 'rites of spring' and how it was mating season. All of nature was turning out to procreate. He could have gone on for a long time, but Nina and Cat had children to get up in the morning and a long drive to school before going to work. Eli only worked mornings at the High Mountain Food Cooperative so that he could be home for the children in the afternoon. If any of them had a cold or had to be home, he could just call in and they were fine with that, unlike Cat and Nina's jobs.

But, as it turned out, Cat decided to call in sick anyway, and Nina drove the children to school in the Jeep because of the conditions of the road. The alternating freeze and thaw process had created ruts that were predicting a nasty mud season should the snow ever melt.

Cat had taken her coffee onto the porch after everyone had left, and the wonderful, but unusual quiet, enveloped her soothingly. She was wrapped in a large, old, Indian blanket that was at the farm when she and Daniel bought it, which now seemed so long ago. Sitting on an old rocking chair, she leaned her head back.

She remembered during those first months of living on the farm when she had hoped she would be able to show that it was important for their daughters to learn more about life than what the city had to offer. Cat had thought that gardening, and living closer to the earth, and having neighbors (although the closest one was an 87-year-old woman more than a mile away), and church suppers, and town meetings, would all be enriching experiences for them. Sometime over the summer, Catherine had stopped to introduce herself and her daughters to Mrs. Wainwright.

"Come back for tea and cookies with the girls!" she said. Cat relished the chance to find out about Mrs. Wainwright's earlier life in the country, how she had lived, what it had *really* been like at that time.

Cat remembered the day well. It was one afternoon when the sun was peeking through clouds, and the birds were singing their hearts out all around the meadow behind the 1800's cape home. As she entered through the front door with Laura and Rebecca, black and white photographs lined the hallway looking like generations of family pictures. The bottom row was in color of mostly young children and looked like pictures from school.

The girls stopped and peered up at the photographs of children at various ages.

"Are those your children?" asked Laura.

"Yes, that's all of them! All in a row!" answered Mrs. Wainwright.

Mrs. Wainwright had had twelve children. Cat wanted very much to ask her questions about her life, her family, and her experiences but didn't want to pry or seem nosy.

They sat in the living room on overstuffed chairs covered in printed fabric, soft and worn. A simple tray with a teapot and mismatched teacups and saucers was set on a low table. A small plate of oatmeal cookies was offered to the girls.

"Have some cookies, girls, they're fresh today."

At the same time, Laura and Rebecca chimed, "Thank you."

Mrs. Wainwright smiled.

"Do you mind if I ask you about your life, Mrs. Wainwright?" began Cat.

"No, child, not a't'all," Mrs. Wainwright replied, "but I'm afraid it wasn't very interesting."

"Oh, your life looks very interesting to me. You raised your own food, you had a lot of children, you've—you've lived here for so many years." In her mind, Cat romanticized those days when people lived on the land, raised their own cows and chickens, and grew their own food. The images were not unlike some movies she had seen when women were sewing their clothes, having quilting bees, wearing bonnets to church suppers.

She continued, "When you were married, did you think you would ever have so many children?" Cat asked.

"Didn't have much choice, then, you know. You got what you got, and of course not all of them lived very long."

"Oh, I'm so sorry, I didn't mean—" Cat began.

Waving her hand, Mrs. Wainwright said, "In those days, you lost a few at birth some times. It just happened. Or when they were two or three years old and came down with scarlet fever and whooping cough. We didn't have vaccinations or the kinds of things you all have now. We needed a big family to run the farm, too. The children worked alongside of us every day. Some of them barely finished sixth grade."

"Oh." Cat said, feeling a bit confused, as this didn't sound like she had pictured it. In her mind, it was more like *Little House on the Prairie*—only in the smaller mountains of New England.

"And later, when my husband got sick, I had to sell off the cows to pay for the doctor bills and the taxes. Couldn't keep afloat by myself even with help from the kids who were still around."

"Oh." Cat said again, beginning to see another chink in her idea of how it was. The girls were playing with their teacups and saucers and asked if they could have another cookie.

"Sure, go ahead," said Mrs. Wainwright. "They'll just get stale if they don't get eaten up now. None-a my kin hardly ever come to visit."

"Well, it must have been wonderfully satisfying, though, working at home and raising your own food—"

"Wonderful, no, and not very satisfying neither. When my husband took sick, it was years before he finally died. I had to take in laundry to make ends meet while taking care of him day and night, night and day," Mrs. Wainwright was shaking her head side-to-side with the memories.

"Most of the kids were married by then and had plenty of young-uns of their own. T'weren't much help. Then just after my husband died, one of my son's took sick and came back home to be taken care of 'til he died." She stopped and shook her head again. "I spent my whole life taking care of other people."

Cat didn't know what to say. She wanted to find something good, and real, and valuable in being able to live so close to the earth as Mrs. Wainwright had done. There had to be some redeeming qualities to a life lived for your home and family.

"Well, you must have had some happy times in all your years, harvesting the crops, knowing you grew your own food, holidays with the family all together and Christmas—"

"Nahhh, half of them weren't around as soon as they got old enough to leave. They wanted to do other things, live their own lives, and join the service." After a pause, Mrs. Wainwright continued, "It wasn't worth it."

"What?" Cat spluttered.

"No way to spend your whole life, jus' takin' care of everyone else and never living yourself."

"Well, well, thank you, Mrs. Wainwright for the tea and cookies. And—and for sharing your life with me. Well, Laura, Rebecca, time to go home now—it's getting late."

Laura and Rebecca looked up at her, each with half a cookie in hand, oblivious to the whole conversation.

Cat hoped she could explain to Laura and Becky what she felt in her heart about how wonderful it was to live in the country, but now she had to rethink it. Of course, she wasn't going to have any more children, and she probably would never farm or have animals. Maybe that was it. Maybe the farm idea should definitely be ruled out. She had told Daniel as soon as he returned on the weekend what Mrs. Wainwright told her.

"See," Daniel said, using Mrs. Wainwright's hard life as reason to leave. "This isn't all it's cracked up to be, Catherine. This is all right to visit, but you really shouldn't live here full-time."

Daniel's attorneys had just called hers after Laura and Becky innocently told him about all the people living at the farm. Attorney Farley had telephoned her to ask, "What the hell is going on there?"

Cat had explained that a few friends had moved in and that everything was under control. Still, she knew she was pushing the envelope even if they only partied when the children were away. No one was giving up smoking pot any time soon. While there would still be more battles to fight, she was relatively safe for a little while longer.

She was lost in the thoughts of the past and precariousness of her future when she noticed two bobbing heads coming up the hill. They were carrying bongo drums.

They could only be looking for her or someone else who lived here.

"Hallo! Hallo!" One of the bobbing heads began calling out, "Is this Cradle Commune? I knew we'd find you! We've been traveling for days!"

"Oh shit," Catherine said softly, "who could these people be?"

The bongo-carrying Kentucky brothers, Bobby Ray and Bobby Joe had hitchhiked from Connecticut after their VW van had broken down and they had run out of money to fix it. Catherine suspected that had run out of gas, but she kept her thoughts to herself.

Fifty feet before they were at the front porch, Bobby Ray introduced himself.

"Hi! I'm Bobby Ray and this here's my brother, Bobby Joe!" Huffing and puffing, up the hill they walked, wide smiles on their sweaty faces.

Catching their breath, they stopped on the bottom stair, panting.

"We're hoping to stay here and live on a real commune! We heard about it in Connecticut and we would work on the farm. We both know how to cut wood and carry water...." began Bobby Ray.

"And, we play bongo drums, too!" added Bobby Joe. Bonus.

Cat had to let them down quickly about their ideas.

"It's not that kind of commune," Cat said. "We all work at jobs and this will be the first year we can put in a garden. We don't have any funds for supporting other people. Everyone has to pay their own way."

Their hopeful, boyish faces fell. They had not received the response they were hoping for.

Cat continued, "And, some of us have children, and the house is electrically heated, so we all have to chip in for the heat as well. We have to buy our groceries at the food cooperative. I don't know if it's ever going to become a working commune. I'm sorry."

The two brothers sat on the front steps, exhausted and hungry from their long journey, and looked at each other.

"What are we going to do, Bobby Ray?" asked the younger brother, Bobby Joe.

"I don't know." Bobby Ray looked down at his feet, and pulled on his bootlaces with both hands. They both looked beat in their patched parkas and bandanas, rucksacks slung over their shoulders. Their cheeks were like red apples from the climb, but Cat knew they would be chilled once they cooled down.

"Well, we can feed you, let you use the phone and you can crash here tonight so that you can make your plans—

perhaps to return to Kentucky? I'm sorry but that's really all we can do," Cat said. She stood up and beckoned for them to follow her inside, then asked "And, how did you hear about this place?"

"My second cousin on my mama's side has a friend at the University of Connecticut and—"

"Oh, no! Not UConn! I hope no one else has the bright idea that we are a real commune!" she said, cutting them off.

She wondered who Lenora and Eli were talking to lately, then thought about Nina probably wanting to keep these guys on, but she would have to dissuade her. There weren't any more separate bedrooms and besides, they couldn't afford to have other people living there who couldn't pay their own way.

Bobby Joe shook his head side-to-side as he followed behind her into the house. Bobby Ray came after. She brought them into the kitchen and put on a pot for tea.

While they sat at the kitchen table Bobby Ray asked, "When do y'all get spring around here?"

"Hard to say," Cat replied, shaking her head, "obviously not yet."

...All I needed was a friend to lend a guiding hand
But you turned into a lover and
Mother what a lover, you wore me out...
Maggie I wish I'd never seen your face...

Rod Stewart and Martin Quittenton
"Maggie May," *Every Picture Tells A Story,* 1971

Chapter 8

The dirt roads were smooth and white with new snow as they led to the Cradle Commune from the highway. The storm had covered the crocuses vying for the sun and turned all of Vermont's mountains white again.

Nina had left on the beginning weekend of April vacation with her boys, who would stay with their father for the week. She would stay in Cambridge with Davy. Eli and Lenora had friends coming up which Cat remembered when she noticed Eli's notes on the calendar. Cat had asked for time off as Daniel was going away and she would get to keep Laura and Becky for the week. They could take skiing lessons every day with all the other school children at Mt. Kenney. Cat was delighted that they would have this chance to stay home with her for once and be able to ski, so she volunteered to assist at the childcare center on the mountain's top. Eli, Lenora, Cat and the girls were having dinner together when everyone arrived from Boston bringing pizza and beer that they had picked up in town.

Eli's friend Mike from UConn had brought his long-time boyhood friend, Tim from Yale. While Mike was in his junior year and was twenty-one, Tim was an eighteen-year-old freshman—the same age as Davy.

Mike was as short and dark as Tim was tall and fair. Mike wore his naturally curly, dark hair to his shoulders. His broad, chunky build made him look like a teddy bear. He was quite a bit shorter than Cat, while Tim was taller, had soft, wavy reddish-blonde hair to his shoulders and a broad face with an open expression. Mike had also brought Lenora's friends, Louisa and Anna. Lenora hadn't seen them since she had moved to the commune last winter, and Louisa and Anna were her friends that she knew from college. Louisa was tall and graceful with beautiful teeth and a warm smile, and Anna was built like Lenora, a good-sized young woman who looked like she could handle anything. Louisa was more outgoing while Anna seemed a little shy, but after introductions, they began asking about what it was like to live on a commune.

"*Faux*-commune!" Cat corrected, laughingly.

Anna asked, "Do you do everything together? Like go to places and go out?"

"Not really," said Cat. "We all have different work schedules and then we have to get the children to school."

"Are you going to grow a garden and become self-sufficient?" asked Louisa.

"I doubt it. We may have a garden, but this house will have to be sold when my divorce is settled."

Cat needed to get the girls ready for bed, so she said they would talk more later, and excused herself with her daughters.

"Time for tubbie!" she said.

The girls didn't want to leave all the new people and all the talking and laughing going on around them.

"Oh, do we have to?" asked Laura.

"We have to," said Cat, "but we'll also have a fun story time!"

"All right," said Laura, not convinced that it would be more fun.

The girls were in the bathroom, having been bathed, and Cat was wrapping them in big towels to dry off, when there was a knock on the bathroom door.

"Yes?"

'It's me, Eli."

"Oh, come in," said Cat.

Eli flounced in, as he would do when he was agitated, and sat on the toilet seat to chat.

"Well," he began, "you have no idea what Mike has up his sleeve."

Cat looked away from the girls, smiled, and said, "What?"

"Mike thinks because he's allllways been gay, and because Tim is having a hard time adjusting to college life, that maybe Tim is really gay, too."

"That's it? I mean, this is what has you all hot and bothered?"

"Well, I think Tim's very cute, but Mike thinks he should have the first—umm," Eli became aware that he was talking in front of the children, "experience with him."

"Hmmm, what does Tim think?"

"Just that he wasn't prepared for what college is like and he's having a hard time getting laid—err, getting dates, so Mike thinks he's looking at the wrong sex." Eli remembered to check himself again.

"Eli, this is about you and Lenora having friends up from school that you haven't seen in a long time. Not about forcing someone to come out."

"I know, I know, I just haven't seen Mike so *concerned.*"

Cat helped the girls into their pajamas and walked them to their room with Eli trailing behind.

Laura asked, "Momma, can Eli read to us?"

Rebecca chimed in, "Oh, please, please, please?"

Cat smiled, "Okay, okay, but you have to ask Eli because his friends are here to see him."

Eli beamed; he loved when the children wanted him to read to them, or be helped into their boots, or reach a toy on a high shelf. He was putty in their hands.

"Oh, yes I will, my babies," he smiled.

"Eli, we're not babies," Laura said, pulling herself up to her full, six-year-old stature.

"I know, I just like to think of all of you as my babies," Eli said. "You may well be the only children I will ever have." Eli shot a soulful glance at Cat.

She smiled back, shaking her head. "Oh, Eli, you are such a trip."

The girls jumped into the big bed they shared and got under the covers, and stacked the pillows against the headboard for Eli to lean against.

He held an imaginary book in his hands and began, "Once upon a time..."

"You don't have a book! You don't have a book!"

They all laughed. "Pick out your favorite book in the whole world," Eli said.

"Then you'll have to read two 'cause Becky and I don't like the same books!" said Laura.

"Nobody likes a smarty pants!" countered Eli.

"I do! I do!" laughed Becky and the silliness and giggles could be heard all through the hallway.

After each girl picked out one book, Eli settled them down to be read to.

"Why is your skin so tan?" asked Becky.

"Cause I am soooooo special," said Eli.

"Rebecca," said Laura, "you always ask Eli that. He came from a country where they needed darker skin to be able to be in the sun."

"Not me," said Eli. "When I was born, my skin was green. It didn't turn brown till I was seven."

"No, sir!" said Laura.

"Really?" said Becky.

Cat descended the back staircase to the kitchen arriving in time to catch snippets of Mike's conversation with Tim.

"Tim, all these problems might be because you are gay."

"That's not it, Mike," said Tim.

"Hi, guys," Cat said, wanting to make her presence known.

She went over to the kitchen cupboard where the mugs were and opened it. Tucked to the side was a coffee mug of rolled joints.

"Want a joint?" Cat said as she walked toward the family room.

"Sure," both Tim and Mike replied and they followed Cat to where Lenora, Louisa and Anna already were.

Soon, Eli joined them and they were passing around the mellow marijuana that Eddie had brought up on his last visit. Lenora was telling Anna and Louisa about all the different people who had been at the farm to party or lived there over the past months since she had arrived. She talked about Christmas, New Years, and the relationships that had formed and then unformed.

Louisa asked, "Lenora, are you and Eli the only gay people on the farm?"

"Yes," Lenora smiled, "though I've certainly tried to change that."

Everyone laughed.

Lenora turned to Cat, "Why don't you join us tonight and sleep in the loft?"

"Nawwww, I don't think so," Cat smiled.

"Oh, come on," said, Anna, "find out what real sex is like."

"That's okay," Cat said, "I'm a flaming hetero and nothing can be done about it."

Lenora tried again to convince Cat when Tim spoke up, "Hey, lay off. She said 'no.'"

Everyone stared at Tim.

"Thanks," Cat said and everyone laughed. Tim blushed. Cat thought he was terribly good-looking in a boyish way, and very nicely put together. His Yale t-shirt barely hid his muscular physique.

Mike said tauntingly, "Well, Tim, you could sleep with Eli and me tonight and see what comes up."

Eli added, "Do you think you're repressing your true self, Tim, because—"

Cat interrupted, "Cookies anyone? I have a dozen or more in the pantry that Eli baked yesterday." After smoking joints for an hour, the munchies were beginning to set in.

"Yeah, let's get some cookies," Tim said, and they all began to file into the kitchen. Tim followed Cat into the pantry to help, and said, "Thanks, Cat."

Cat smiled up at Tim and her eyes traced the fullness of his curved lips.

"You are welcome."

Tim noticed Cat's nipples through her t-shirt and felt a surge of energy. As he turned away to re-enter the kitchen, Cat looked at how his jeans shaped around his butt. She brought the large tin out of the pantry and placed it on the kitchen table. Eli got the cans of beer out of the refrigerator.

Everyone was milling around the kitchen with a good buzz on and Mike, while swigging down a beer and filling his mouth with cookies, was starting up the conversation about Tim's denial of being a *potential* homosexual.

Tim noticed the calendar on the cellar door in the kitchen and walked over to it. He saw the day's date with his name written along with the other visitors.

Eli noticed his interest and interjected, "That's my social calendar. I like to keep track of who's coming and who's going."

Anna held a cookie in her mouth and passed it with her teeth to Lenora so Lenora would take it from her. Then, Lenora kissed her. Cat was glad the girls had gone to bed.

Tim glanced at Cat while he said, "I'm glad I made it on your social calendar."

Cat smiled back at Tim.

Eli said that maybe Tim was just shy at school, sounding more like he was willing to cut Tim some slack.

Tim said something about his lack of experience.

"Are you still a virgin?" Mike demanded.

Tim flushed to the roots of his hair and looked like he was breaking a sweat. "Something like that," he mumbled.

"Ohh, Tim," everyone began to chant, "Tim's a virgin! Tim's a virgin!"

Cat walked over to Tim, wrapped her arms around his neck and kissed him firmly on the mouth.

"What the fuck?" Mike started.

"Hey, let's go listen to some music. I've got *The Low-Spark of High-Heeled Boys*, by Traffic," said Eli. "I've got albums by Procul Harem, David Bowie's *The Rise and Fall of Ziggie Stardust*, and Bob Marley, too."

Mike was still shaking his head as he turned to follow Eli with everyone else.

They all returned to the family room, closed the door and left Cat and Tim in the kitchen. Cat and Tim were in a lip lock while hugging each other tightly, Cat having pushed Tim against the cellar door for better leverage.

After what seemed to be quite awhile of making out, stroking and fondling each other, Tim had reached under Cat's t-shirt to touch her naked breasts.

Cat was getting pretty hot, and took Tim's hand to lead him up the front stairs to her bedroom.

While she began to undress him, she said, "You are going to have such a good time Tim, there's nothing to worry about." Cat smiled while she pulled his t-shirt over his head and breathed in his warm, musky smell. She kissed his chest and neck and he pulled her close to him so he could push against her. She could feel his heat through his jeans.

"Wait a second," Cat said, "I need to check on my girls and be sure they are asleep."

"Okay," Tim grinned. "I'll wait right here," and sat down on Cat's bed. When she left, he looked around the room with the flowery wallpaper that went up over the ceiling. The white-painted wood floors and the antique bureau with lace cloth on it seemed very feminine. Here he was at this commune in a bedroom that looked nothing like the tie-dye styles and Indian bedspreads he had seen at college. Tim didn't know for sure, but he bet other communal farms didn't look like this one. There were bottles of nail polish in pink and frosted colors on the bureau. A straw hat hung on the back of the bedroom door with a ribbon band that trailed from it in cream silk. Her bed had a white quilt that was over cream and pink colored blankets with satin edges. Her pillows were white with lace edges, and there were at least six of them. A very soft throw at the foot of the bed was decorated with large stuffed animals. Tim wondered if she slept with all of this stuff on her bed at night or if it was just when the bed was made. He leaned back on the pillows and realized there was a mirror mounted on the slanted ceiling overhead and he could see himself.

Cat went to the back of the house where the children's bedrooms were. With Nina's boys away, Eli and Mike could sleep in the boys' bed but Cat hoped they would all stay in the family room. The loft had plenty of room as well as the sofas by the fireplace. She looked in at her sleeping girls and they were both breathing deeply. She was glad because she didn't like having anyone in her bed when her girls were home. She worried they would wake up and come into her bedroom at night and be confused or upset to see her in bed with someone other than their father.

She closed their door all the way, and the dividing hall door that would hopefully maintain peace and quiet in the upstairs from the music being played in the family room. She then returned to the front of the house and closed her bedroom door.

Tim was already in bed, his clothes on the floor.

"No fair," Cat said. "You didn't let me undress you!" She feigned disappointment.

Tim looked shy, the covers pulled up to his armpits.

Standing in front of him with the bedside light on, she peeled off her t-shirt exposing her well-shaped breasts. Then, she kicked off her Dr. Scholl's sandals, and slowly unbuttoned her Levi jeans before dropping them to the floor while moving her hips suggestively. She didn't have on any underwear. Her curvaceous hips and smooth stomach were making Tim's heart beat faster, and he dared not stare below that. Tim's expression looked like a kid on Christmas morning who found the present he wanted under the tree.

She pulled back the covers and slid in next to him.

...Now, I really want to see you (hare rama)
Really want to be with you (hare rama)
Really want to see you lord (aaah)
But it takes so long, my lord (hallelujah)...

George Harrison,
"My Sweet Lord," *Concert for Bangladesh*, 1971

Chapter 9

Spring finally arrived in a form that Cat wasn't used to. There were no forsythias, the crocuses had come and gone, and the daffodils were still surrounded by snow. Everyone on the farm had planned to plant a garden and had just learned that the only way to do that was to start all the plants inside. They would have to wait until after the last frost—in June—to be able to actually put the seedlings in the ground. When they learned that they could start them in the barn, they thought they were all set.

Eli, Davy and Nina organized the worktable under a triple-fluorescent light that ran the whole length of one wall. Lenora and Cat sorted the packages of organic seeds that Lenora had insisted on getting and read instructions from gardening books that Jessica and Gene had loaned them. Gene's cousin, Scott, had been staying at the log cabin off and on—ever since January's gathering. He visited the commune frequently and seemed very interested in what they were doing. One night, sitting around the family room listening to Rod Stewart and Procul Harem albums, Scott brought up other possible uses for the spacious barn.

"You could grow some nice weed there," he said.

"No," Cat quickly replied, "I can't take any chances with my husband still trying to prove me an unfit mother. No way."

When everyone else agreed with Scott, Nina took Cat's side—for once. "You haven't been through what Cat went through over her divorce. You have no idea what can happen."

Over the next couple of weeks, Scott was spending more and more weekend time at the farm, and Eli was adding his name to the calendar for the times he was coming over for the evening.

While cooking supper one night, Eli asked Cat, "Are you interested in Scott? 'Cause you guys seem to circle around each other a lot."

"I don't know," Cat said, looking away.

"What about Tim? He says he's been writing you and you never respond."

"I know. He's just too young." Cat replied, sheepishly, feeling guilty that she had slept with him and then didn't want to see him again.

"He's in love with you, you know," Eli said, as if being Tim's protector.

"So now you want Tim to be a heterosexual?" Cat tried to joke with Eli.

"Well, you did spend a week with him," said Eli.

"And that's all it was. A week of nights after spending the days with the girls skiing at Mt. Kenney and volunteering at the day care center."

"As I remember, Tim worked as a volunteer at the day care center too."

"Yup, and he was great at it. And I really, really thanked him."

"Phoo on you!" Eli said, acting miffed. "Someday you'll fall in love and you won't be able to have who you want."

Cat smiled and shrugged her shoulders.

That evening, Scott came with some new albums to listen to that he had brought from a trip to his Cambridge apartment. There wasn't a store in town that carried record albums so unless Davy brought them, they couldn't easily get all the new music except on the sometimes-working radio.

After dinner, when the children were put to bed, everyone sat in the family room sharing joints and listening to the Rolling Stones album, *Sticky Fingers*. Cat was looking forward to the new Aerosmith album but still enjoyed their first one with her favorite songs, "Dream On" and "Mama Kin". Nina and Cat were talking about when the children would have to leave for the summer and the arrangements that they would make. Then they played Stevie Wonder's album, *Music of My Mind*, singing along in a mild euphoric buzz, "boom, boom, boom, I love you..." Davy's speakers sounded great but Cat had to check from the kitchen to be sure it wasn't too loud for the children upstairs.

When she went into the hallway, Scott followed along behind her. As she turned to close the door, he reached for her and kissed her lightly on the mouth.

"Ohh," Cat said, surprised, eyes wide open.

Scott laughed and kept his hands around her waist.

"No, Scott, it's just not the right time."

"Well—let me know when it is," Scott replied, smiling.

Cat nodded and turned around toward the kitchen with a slight frown.

Scott returned to the family room and closed the door behind him. Then, Cat went up the back stairs and checked the children's bedrooms. All were fast asleep.

On the weekend, with the children home from school, Cat and Nina took them into the barn to see all the little pots with seeds and seedlings that they had planted. They explained that the growing season started late where they lived, but when everyone returned after the summer, there would still be lots of things for them to see.

"We'll have good food we grow ourselves," said Nina. "We'll have lettuce and broccoli and corn-on-the-cob!"

"Yes," added Cat, "maybe we can even have some all winter if we learn how to store it."

"The freezer," said Nina. "Canning just removes nutrients, it's better to quickly blanch fresh food and freeze it."

"Have you been talking to Lenora?" asked Cat.

Nina laughed. The children looked at the little green shoots coming out of some of the pots. This is what Cat had been hoping to have happen—a garden in their backyard with fresh vegetables to pick and eat. She wondered if they would remember any of this once they left for the summer with their fathers, grandparents and all their old friends at their summer camp.

Cat and Nina had been preparing the children for leaving in June, and both said they would call them Sundays and visit once or twice. It would be a bit easier for Nina as she could stay with her in-laws at their summer home and be with her children. So many things were unresolved. Cat wasn't looking forward to June.

After the children were put to bed, Cat went out on the front porch alone and sipped some mint tea while she mulled over the changes in her life. The copper bush that she had placed in the shrubs was green, and some areas looked rusty. Sounds of the Crosby, Stills, Nash & Young album, *Déjà Vu,* drifted in the background of her thoughts. Once she believed that this would be a "very, very, very fine house." Now she wondered what the future would hold for her and her children. Perhaps she was meant to be alone, to never find anyone to love who would understand her—or who she would understand.

As soon as school closed, she would have to drive her daughters to their father's for the summer. She would have to pack their clothes up, an idea which still filled her with dread. She would always be fearful about getting Laura and Becky back. She hoped her old nightmares wouldn't return about losing them. She hoped Daniel wouldn't say things to frighten the girls or turn them against her, but there was nothing she could do about that. She always held them in her thoughts before going to bed at night, her way of praying for their safety and to send them her love. Trying to meditate in the morning was a challenge with all the activity and preparations for work and school. Perhaps over the summer, when the commune was quieter, she could make it part of her daily, if not morning, ritual—like preparing her coffee.

Nina appeared in the doorway to the porch.

"Hey, girl, whatcha doing?" she asked, holding the screen door open.

"Just thinking," said Cat.

"Bad idea, come on in the family room, we're getting stoned."

"Good idea!" Cat smiled up at Nina, stood and followed her into the house.

The next day when Eli returned from the health food store, he had a flyer that said Ram Dass, a spiritual guru, was going to be speaking in New Hampshire. It wasn't too far away to make a day trip.

"Look who is going to be in New Hampshire this coming weekend!"

"Who?" asked Cat.

"Ram Dass! That's who! We have to take the babies and go!"

"Why? Who's Ram Dass?"

"Oh, darling girl, he wrote *Be Here Now*, it's practically the new Bible! He used to be a Harvard professor. Don't tell me you never heard of him?"

"Didn't he take LSD with Timothy Leary?"

"Yes, yes, but that was all before he met his spiritual teacher, Neem Karoli Baba. After his time of study, Ram Dass said there is no drug that can do for you what meditation can do."

"Really?"

"Really. Let's all go. You will get so high from being in his presence, you won't believe you're not on acid."

"Believe me, I am never taking acid. But, all right. Let's take the kids and go."

After another hectic week of work and school, Saturday morning arrived bright and clear. At the breakfast table, Cat felt a bit of electricity as everyone became involved in the discussion about Ram Dass.

"We should all dress in white," said Eli.

"Aww, come on, Eli," said Lenora.

Cat knew of a few things she could wear. She had a white shirt made in India that she had bought when she still lived in Boston. She took the girls back upstairs to change. A few minutes later, she returned and they discussed the logistics of who would go in the Datsun and who would go in the Jeep.

Nina didn't think it was all that important to wear white, so she and Davy gathered the boys up to get ready to go.

"We should leave; it's going to take at least two hours to get there."

Lenora went with Nina, Davy, Erin and Nathan. Eli went with Cat, Laura and Becky.

When they arrived, there was an area where other cars were parked. Then they walked up to the house that was set back and looked like a turn-of-the-century summer home. When they entered, there was a room with chairs lined up in rows. A gray-haired, bearded man was sitting cross-legged at the front of the room.

"Is that Ram Dass?" asked Cat.

Eli nodded.

Their group took up a row of chairs. There were about ten other people. Soon, more people arrived and sat down. There was a quiet expectancy that filled the room until Ram Dass opened his eyes, looked over the people, smiled and began to speak.

The tone of his voice, his storytelling about his own spiritual journey and his humor lifted Cat up in a way she had not experienced before. He led them through a meditation and even the children were enthralled.

Then he led them into a round of singing:

"Listen, listen listen to my heart song
Listen, listen listen to my heart song
I will never forget you. I will never forsake you.
I will never forget you. I will never forsake you..."[12]

At the end of the gathering, Ram Dass announced that he would hug anyone who wanted to be hugged. Beaming faces nodded and began to get in line.

"I want to hug Ram Dass," said Cat.

"Me, too," said Eli.

"Yeah, I want to," said Lenora.

The kids hung back, uncertain.

"Davy and I will wait outside," said Nina.

They took all the children outside with them while Eli, Cat and Lenora stood in line for their turn. Cat had never experienced such a blissful hug. Between the high of the group meditation, shared singing, and Ram Dass's hug, Cat felt like she was floating on air.

The met up outside and walked to the cars. Nina offered Cat a joint for the ride home.

"No thanks, I don't want to change how I am feeling right now."

Nina knew Cat didn't smoke in front of her daughters, but they were already lighting up. Cat knew that she couldn't get any higher no matter what she took.

"It won't last," said Eli.

"I guess not, but it's the best feeling I have ever known," said Cat.

SUMMER 1975

...But it's too late, baby, now it's too late
though we really did try to make it.
Somethin' inside has died, and I can't hide,
and I just can't fake it, oh, no, no...

Carole King and Toni Stern,
"It's Too Late," *Tapestry,* 1971

Chapter 10

Catherine returned from driving her daughters to Daniel's home in Boston for summer vacation. She felt weak and shaky with emotion, crying all the way back to the commune, and she knew she would dread seeing their empty bedroom. The memories of having her daughters taken away were still too fresh in her mind. She could visit them once during the two months—but she didn't know if she could handle it, if she could keep leaving them. If she became upset in front of them, it would be bad for her daughters. If she didn't visit them, it would seem that she didn't want to see them. Back and forth, back and forth like a ping pong ball, her unsolvable feelings flipped-flopped inside her. She was looking forward to some time alone at the commune. *Farm,* she corrected herself. *We're starting a real garden. It will be a farm.*

Nina had driven her boys to Maine and would visit her in-laws there for a week before driving on to New York to visit her parents.

Eli returned to Connecticut to apply for a summer theater position having been turned down at the Grande Blanc theater group. He couldn't believe he wasn't hired after all the attention he had received since he was the only gay, black man for at least one hundred miles. Lenora, too, had left to work on a women's rights project in Cambridge, and Jessica and Gene were nearly settled into their log cabin, only visiting once in awhile.

Cat had time off from working at the store. The owner's daughter was home from college and they offered Cat a break, if she wanted it, for the last two weeks of June. Cat jumped at the opportunity. She had begun to long for the peace and quiet the beautiful environment could provide. Her fantasy idea of living with friends and so many people coming and going had gotten old. This would be the first time she was really alone since those earlier dark days when she didn't want to be. With all the children away, the house empty, the absolute uninterrupted quiet began to lull Cat into a peacefulness she hadn't felt in a long time.

She thought of the Summer Solstice, which meant the turning point when the days would be growing shorter, a fact she very much disliked. Her favorite season was summer with its long days of light and days of warmth. She would have liked the sun to set at 10:00 or 11:00 p.m. and extend the length of day even further. Maybe there would be time to go to the lake and sit in the sun. Or, start a knitting project. Or, just read and relax.

Cat made some salad for supper, poured a tall glass of lemonade that Eli had fresh-squeezed before leaving, and brought it outside to the front porch. She lit the punk incense to deter the mosquitoes that would arrive at dusk, and enjoyed taking in the scenes around her beautiful home. To her left, an open meadow rolled away where once a herd of cows would have been grazing. Behind the house, an old cow path led down to an area now grown over with small trees and scrubby underbrush. To her right, a u-shaped side yard lay, made by the adjoining family room between house and barn. Beyond the barn, another meadow wrapped around it and across the back of the house, rising up the hill like surrounding arms.

As Cat looked across the road, the partially open view allowed her to see an edge of the Green Mountains. The huge maples that bordered the dirt road which passed in front of the yard continued as if marching along their parallel path. She could see part way down the road to the left where the maples zigzagged off into the distance. She remembered driving up the road the first time and staring up at the tall arbor of leaves that crossed overhead. A feeling of peace and protection had swept over her.

The dappling of the leaf shadows reminded her of her backyard in early childhood. She had sat within a giant gaggle of lilac bushes that had passed blooming one hot, summer day and noticed the leaf shadows on her chubby-child bare arms and legs. At kindergarten, they were learning to use little rubber stamps and she knew her father had a stamp pad on his desk. She went into the house, found the black, indelible ink stamp pad, and went back outside to sit on the cool damp earth within the bushes. She carefully opened the stamp pad, picked up some leaves, and pressed them onto the pad carefully with her little fingers. She looked to see if the ink had transferred to the leaf. Satisfied, she matched the shadows from the leaves on her arms and legs by pressing the leaf on them, effectively leaf-patterning herself with black, indelible ink. Cat smiled, remembering her mother's horrified expression when she had proudly walked into the kitchen to show her.

I must have forgotten to instruct Laura and Becky how to do that one, Cat thought.

The sun was setting and she could just make out the soft gold and crimson colors in the far distance as it hid behind the mountain's edge. Her thoughts drifted: *Ideally, I could stay here and buy the land across the road and open up the old meadow again. I bet there would a better view of the mountains—maybe I could actually see the sunset.*

She didn't expect to sleep well her first night alone without her daughters, but she went inside and made a mug of lukewarm milk with honey and cinnamon to assist her in settling down. Even in the heat of summer, most evenings were pleasantly cool and she would find herself reaching for a blanket to wrap up in. When she walked from the kitchen to the family room, the house sounded hollow, and her Dr. Scholl's sandals made more noise on the old wood floors than she usually noticed.

As she entered the family room, Cat looked at the bookshelves along the walls for something to read. Everyone had contributed to the bookshelves that lined one entire wall, separated by the three windows.

Urantia was more than she could handle tonight, she thought, scanning among the titles, then realized they had been filed alphabetically. "Wow!" Cat exclaimed out loud, breaking the silence and creating a mild echo. Perhaps Eli, in a cleaning fit, had done this when his "babies" were at school.

Cat began to look again, the Carlos Castaneda books were lined up, but she had already read them and not that long ago. The Dune trilogy was there, and she remembered everyone seemed to be talking about it lately. Davy loved the *The Fellowship of the Ring* by J.R.R. Tolkein. And, of course, Ram Dass's bestseller, *Be Here Now* was read and often quoted by everyone. Lenora had contributed all the feminist literature including *Our Bodies, Our Selves,* books about Elizabeth Cady Stanton, and some *Ms.* Magazines.[13] But Cat wanted something a bit lighter. Finally, she came upon Kurt Vonnegut's books, and selected *Slaughterhouse-Five* because of her attraction to the Tralfamadorians. In this science fiction look at other life forms, Tralfamadorians are able to see into four dimensions, which Cat wished she did so she could know how her divorce would turn out. She locked the family room door to the barn and to the outside, picked up her mug of warm milk, and went up the back staircase to cross through the kids' hallway.

Cat averted her eyes until she was in the front section of the house where her bedroom was and did not allow herself to look into Laura and Becky's bedroom.

She plumped up her pillows and began to read, drifted off to sleep and then awoke to turn off her reading light. It was pitch dark, no moonlight at all. *Perhaps it's going to rain,* Cat mused as she fell into the deep sleep of the very tired.

Cat's eyes shot open as sounds of a loud horn blasted her awake. She sat up in bed. Lights angled from below were shining into her bedroom window on the ceiling.

Confused, she staggered to the side of the window, but she was blinded by the lights and could only make out the shape of a truck that had driven up onto the lawn in front of the porch below. She heard the sounds of men's voices yelling:

"Hey Cat! Hey Kitty-Kitty-Cat!" They hollered and laughed, and flicked the truck's high beams off and on while tooting the horn.

"We've got lots of beer out here!" said one.

"Yeah, come on out and drink with us!" yelled another.

Cat began shaking in the dark like a wet animal. She slowly backed away from the side of the window so she wouldn't be seen, and crept in the dark to the back of the house. Her heart was pounding as she felt her way down the back staircase to the kitchen below where the telephone hung on the hall wall. She didn't know the local police number; only the fire department number was stuck on the side of the telephone. She didn't dare put on the lights as she hoped they might think she wasn't home, even though her Jeep was parked in the side yard. She knew this late at night it would be hard to rouse the local operator, but that was all she could think of to do.

Unexpectedly, the racket grew louder, and she heard glass breaking and then swearing.

"Shit, look at what you did, you asshole!" yelled one of the men.

Cat began to think of where she could hide if they tried to come in. Even if she got the operator, it would be a long time until the deputy got there. The dirt floor cellar would be damp and filled with spiders. The barn? No, no, she needed to be able to get outside and the only doors that opened would be right into the side yard in full view of where they were. Then, she remembered the odd door upstairs, a door that led outside to the back of the house from the second floor that must have once been a way to enter from the back fields. If there were stairs, they were long gone, and Cat had slid a bureau in front of it to prevent the kids from ever opening it by mistake.

She could possibly jump from there, and then go up behind the house where she knew she could hide—if she didn't break her legs jumping—or fall, and make a lot of noise.

As quickly as the plan evolved, her mind racing and body feeling full of adrenalin, she heard the metallic crunch of gears shifting and the truck backing away from the front lawn.

"If I get a flat tire—" she heard as they drove away and the words trailed off.

She walked to the front of the house and checked the front door. It wasn't even locked.

Relief flooded Cat all at once as she first locked the door securely, and then climbed the front stairs to her bedroom. Chilled from flushing with fear, she pulled another blanket out of her closet in the dark, and crawled under the covers. She tried to breathe evenly to calm herself down.

Eventually, she calmed down and fell asleep. She dreamed fitfully of being chased down long corridors that ended abruptly, then turned and lengthened again like some crazy maze. When Catherine awoke, too warm under the extra blankets, her bedroom was filled with light, and the sun was high in the sky. It was almost noon.

That afternoon, Cat went to town to see Pam at Whitey's Restaurant, who hadn't been back to the farm since New Year's Eve. She went after the lunch rush so it would be slow enough to tell Pam about the bad scare she had had the night before, and the details of what had happened. Pam seemed almost amused.

"Oh, probably just a couple good ol' boys looking for a few laughs!" Pam smiled.

"But—but I'm there alone, and people know it, and what if they tried to break in?"

Pam laughed. "I wouldn't worry about it! You could have gone out and had a few beers!"

When Cat left the restaurant, she was thinking about what Pam had said. *Pam probably would have gone outside and drank with them. She probably would have enjoyed it.* She felt totally exasperated with their exchange as she drove back to the farm. After she parked the Jeep in the side yard, she walked around the front lawn where she spotted some broken glass by the side of the road. It was partially buried at the edge of the grass. She gingerly picked it up and carried it inside to the trash can.

The phone rang and it was Heather, someone else she had met at the High Health Food Cooperative. She really liked her a lot but she and her husband, Tom, didn't come to the commune to hang out. It just wasn't their thing. They actually had a viable garden that took up most of their time, and they had also been raising rabbits and chickens.

"Tom and I would like you to come for dinner. I heard you're alone there now from Eli before he left for the summer. We would love to see you."

"That would be super," Cat said, thinking they would provide the sympathetic response that Pam had lacked. And, now that the small plants had been left in her care, Cat thought it would be a good time to pick up some pointers about gardening. She wondered if she would ever be able to learn to grow anything, let alone become self-sufficient.

After dinner, talk turned to how she was doing without the girls for the summer, and the rest of the housemates who had left. She told them the story of the events that occurred night before.

"This truck drove right up on the lawn and shined its lights into the house! It was just awful!"

"Have you got a gun?" asked Tom.

"Well, there's an old shot gun hanging over the mantel, but I've never used it."

"Bring it over," said Tom, "we'll fix you right up."

Driving home later that night, Cat didn't know which scared her more—the "good ol' boys" or the idea of shooting a gun.

When she drove into the dark side yard, she thought, *Why not put the Jeep in the barn?* It would look like she wasn't home.

She walked purposefully into the family room, which wasn't locked as usual, and locked it behind her. Then she walked into the barn through the door at the far end without turning on any lights; she could see by the light of the moon shining through the barn windows. Stepping to the big, barn doors, she grabbed hold of the plank that lay across the metal brackets. Just as she slid it upward, she heard a truck and the sound of distant voices approaching the hill. Letting go of the plank, it slipped back into place. She looked out the small barn window that faced the road.

It was the same truck, a large-tired monstrosity that all the men in the area seemed to own. She watched as they pulled onto the front lawn facing the porch again. Losing her direct line of vision from that angle, she turned and felt the wall so she could climb the stairs to the second floor, and looked out the window facing the inner yard. Now she could make out two men in the truck, drinking beer out of cans this time, and calling her name again, while flicking the high beams on and off so the light would enter the living rooms downstairs and the bedrooms upstairs.

From this vantage point, Cat felt growing anger blooming inside of her. She crept back down the stairs, and felt her way through the shed. She could see fairly well because of the moonlight, and worked her way into the kitchen hallway. She dialed the operator who answered sleepily after more than a dozen rings.

"Operator," she yawned.

"This is Catherine Janson at the old Sheldon farm. Two guys in a pickup truck have driven onto my front lawn, yelling my name and flicking their lights off and on."

"Yes?" the operator answered curtly, as if to say, "So?"

"Can you connect me with the police, please?"

"Are you sure that's necessary? Probably just a couple good ol'---

"Good ol' boys, yes," Cat finished for her.

"You'll be waking up Deputy Shepherd and he has several young-uns," the operator finished.

"I have 'young-uns' of my own," Cat said dryly, "I'll be glad to take responsibility."

After a few moments of clicks, silence and more clicks, an even sleepier Deputy Shepherd was on the line.

"Deputy Shepherd," he stated gruffly.

"Sorry to bother you, Deputy Shepherd," Catherine began, "but this is the second night in a row some men have driven up onto my property, yelling my name, and throwing beer bottles all over my lawn!"

"Huh?"

"Make them go away!" Cat finished.

"Mrs. Janson, by the time I get there, they will probably be gone away. They'll be long gone. It's probably the Miller boys out raising a little hell. Nothing to worry about. It'll pass. Just don't put any lights on."

"What? This is my home!" Cat said, indignantly, but checking her volume. "What if they try to come in?"

"They won't, but, you got a shot gun?"

"Well, yeah, but it's old and I've never fired it, and—"

"Always a good idea in the country to keep a loaded shotgun handy," said Deputy Shepherd. "Just seeing a girl with a gun will scare 'em off!"

"But—but..."

"You'll be fine," and he hung up. She thought she heard a suppressed chuckle.

The men had broken into song, "Won't you come out tonight, come out tonight, come out tonight, and dance by the light of the mooooooo—oon!" Then laughter. They began the "Ten Bottles of Beer on the Wall" song, put the truck into reverse, backed onto the road, and drove away.

The next morning, Cat took down the old shotgun that hung over the fireplace. She brought it to Tom to see if it actually worked. He came in from the fields and took the gun to his work shop where he oiled it, and showed her how to load it. He said it was in good shape considering the fact it had probably been hanging there for a half-century without use. He told her what type of buckshot to buy at the local hardware store.

"You want to scare them, not kill 'em." Tom said.

"I don't?" said Cat, raising an eyebrow.

"You know, you can do some damage with buckshot under the skin. They'll have to go to the doctor's to get it removed—plus, it will hurt like hell!"

"All right," Cat conceded.

She put the gun in the back of the Jeep, wrapped in a blanket, and drove to the hardware store where she bought two boxes of buckshot.

The tall, gangly, long-nosed hardware store owner, Jon Dothan, cocked an eyebrow at Cat.

"Going birding?" he asked, "'Cause it's not birding season yet."

"Nope."

"Target practice?"

"Maybe." Cat wasn't offering any information she didn't have to.

"This here buckshot spreads out pretty wide, 'bout two feet in diameter."

"Then I won't miss my target, will I?" Cat replied, scooping up the boxes as she turned and walked out of the store.

He cast a sideways glance over his long nose, rubbed his jaw as she walked out, thinking, *Wonder what those hippies are up to now?*

That night, Cat loaded her gun and sat on the front porch in the dark with it lying across her lap. She had never shot a gun in her life. Around midnight, she gave up and went to bed. The next night, she sat outside again, just waiting for them to drive up and try to scare her, growing more agitated by the hour. And, again, nothing. She was starting to feel foolish.

The third day, she decided to try some actual target practice in the old cellar hole off the cow path. She set up a beer can from those left on her lawn.

When she shot the gun, it knocked her back a couple of feet, and hurt her shoulder. She steadied herself, and tried again. Now she began to aim lower at the beer can, instead of at it, because the gun always kicked up when she fired it. She still missed it, but the spray from the buckshot hit the can and toppled it over.

"Yeahhhh!" she whooped. She walked over to examine the damage and found that several small, round pieces of buck shot had entered the beer can—there were little, round holes.

"That works," she said aloud, feeling more confident. "At least I'll hit something."

She tried again, never actually centering on the beer can itself, but each time, she sprayed it with those small, round metal balls.

Satisfied, Cat went back to the house to have a bite to eat and lay in wait. Finally, at 10:30 p.m., she went to bed, standing the loaded shotgun next to her night table. Chilled, she put on her white flannel nightgown. *Summer indeed,* she thought. It had grown cooler each evening as if the weather was already marching toward fall.

She had just begun to doze off when the unmistakable sound of an engine, straining up the hill, and the sound of whooping voices could be heard. Cat sat up, wide awake, her long hair, loose and wild around her. She stood up and grabbed the shotgun. She trembled slightly as she tried to confidently walk down the front staircase.

They were parked on the lawn again; reminding her of each time the truck tires had cut through the grass leaving muddy ruts in its wake. The nerve that they would do such a thing made her even angrier. Then she heard them calling her name. They were laughing and flipping empty beer cans into the truck bed behind them, not caring if they landed there, or fell to the ground.

One of the men said, "Gotta take a leak."

The passenger door opened and he jumped down while the driver said, "Hey, get away from my truck, asshole!"

"I'm not pissing on your truck!"

He turned to face the road, his back to the porch, and Cat opened the front door. She stood barefoot on the porch with her white flannel nightgown billowing out behind her, her shoulders surrounded by her long, blonde hair. Her eyes were wild with fear and anger, and she raised her shotgun to her shoulder, aiming at the guy outside of the truck.

"You're trespassing!" Cat yelled.

"Whoaaaa, whoaaaa," the driver leaned out his side, "hang on a minute!" He raised his hand as if to stop her.

"Get off of my property!"

She heard the truck changing gears as it started to roll backwards.

The man was still peeing as he turned quickly to see what was going on, and Cat aimed the gun in his general direction. *I've got one shot*, she thought, pulling the trigger, *this better be good.*

"Yeeeeeeeowwwwwwwww!"

The man was holding his penis with one hand and jumping up and down while reaching for the truck door with the other.

Cat didn't know where she hit him, but she knew he might have caught some of it in his tender parts. He was still howling as they drove off.

"The **AIM Song**[14] is the name given to a Native American intertribal song. Although the song originally did not have a name, it gained its current alias through association with the American Indian Movement..."

Chapter 11

In July, Cheryl and Sam invited everyone at the Cradle Commune to come to a powwow with them. They would be bringing their tepee, and they all would sleep in it. Nina wasn't as interested as Cat was, and Lenora would rather stay at the commune and work on the garden as they had been every weekend. Many of the lettuces and peppers were in full swing, and even the corn looked like it would come up. Working during the week kept everyone pretty busy, and the weekend was really the only time they could take care of encouraging and maintaining the garden. As it was, they had to put a radio in it each night to keep out all the critters that would eat everything, and Cat had made a scarecrow out of some old clothes which she stuffed with hay. They had bought bales of it to put down between the garden rows to hold back the weeds, but there was still plenty of weeding to do. They shook ground red pepper onto the vegetables to keep them from being eaten by all the insects. Cat had never seen so many insects in her life until they had a garden.

Nina and Lenora told Cat to go ahead. They would take care of the garden that weekend, and Davy would be there to help, too. Eli was coming back, and he could help by getting food together and cooking for them while they toiled outside. Eli didn't like being outside that much. Cat contended it was because the bugs and insects thought he was a chocolate bar.

"Very funny," Eli had said. "So why do you try to get a tan?"

The weekend arrived, and Friday night Cat had to prepare for the next morning's trip with Cheryl and Sam who would pick her up at 5:00 a.m. Davy and Eli also arrived Friday night, and Nina and Lenora had music blasting in the family room till after midnight. Cat was too excited to go to sleep as early as she thought she should, but she had hoped to get some rest. She set her alarm for 4:45 a.m. and laid out her jeans and t-shirt. Her sleeping bag was rolled up and stuffed into her backpack with a change of clothes. For all intents and purposes, she was as ready as she would be. She did add a bandana, however, to tie around her hair and keep it back from her face for the drive. She didn't know what to expect and she was looking forward to the new experience.

She awakened just before the alarm went off and quickly dressed, slung her backpack over her shoulder, and headed down the front stairs and out the door to be on the porch. She could hear a rumbling engine, and sure enough, Sam's old International green truck came up the hill with tepee poles lashed across the truck bed rack. They extended four or five feet beyond the end and Sam had tied a red bandana on the longest pole. Cat hoped there was room inside for her.

Sam got out and told her to put her backpack in the truck bed next to theirs, along with the rolled up tepee and blankets. Cat put it down on the metal and hoped it wouldn't rain. The poles made an open roof over the truck bed, and red strips of cloth hung from the ends.

Then, she climbed in next to Cheryl and after a bit of grinding the gear shift, they were off. It took nearly five hours to get to the destination in upstate New York where the gathering of several Native American nations was being held. Cat didn't know what anything meant and had lots of questions for Sam and Cheryl.

When they arrived, they were assigned a place to put up their tepee as part of a very large circle of tepees. The powwow would be held in the center, and those who had arrived earlier were erecting tall poles in a circle and stringing them together with pine boughs. This would define the center area for the powwow festivities and they told Cat that you walked around the circle—not through it. The circle was designated as a sacred gathering place for drumming and dancing.

Cat counted twenty-two erected tepees before she was put to work with Cheryl to tie three poles together and stand them up. Then each of them pulled one of the poles outward to make the circle even. Sam placed the rest of the poles around the three main poles by placing several of them in each section of crossed poles. Once they were spread in a near-perfect circle, from what Cat could tell, the last pole was laid on the ground and Sam tied the tepee canvas to it. As he and Cheryl pulled it up by walking underneath the pole to raise it, the tepee unfurled down around them. Once the last pole was in place, Sam wrapped the tepee around all the poles, and fastened them with small-carved pegs in the front. Cat was amazed at the process, the fact that it wasn't very hard to put it up, and the ease with which it became a real shelter. She helped Cheryl attach the door piece that could be tied open so they could unload the truck and carry in their backpacks, sleeping bags and blankets. In daylight, it was a perfect circle of light. There were front flaps at the top that could be closed together to secure it against rain, and then, by leaving them open, one could view the blue sky through the criss-crossed poles. It was simply beautiful. Cat thrilled at the idea of sleeping in it at night.

Sam brought in a gardening shovel and removed a piece of sod in the center to create a fire pit. Cheryl placed their blankets and bedding at the back of the tepee, which they explained, was the area where the tepee owners slept. Cat placed her backpack along one side and pulled out her sleeping bag and mat.

Now it was time to help everyone else with the construction of the center area for the drum, and clear the ground of sticks and rocks for the dancing that would be held that evening. The women were creating a sideboard out of planks to set up a serving area. Everyone contributed food to help out. Cat wanted to work on the construction but one of the Native men told her to go help the women out. Annoyed, she left the center and went to the tables. Cheryl laughed when Cat told her what had happened.

"No big deal here, Cat! They stick to the old traditions of women working in the home and men working on building and—and you just have to go along with it," Cheryl said, laughingly. "Some of the younger Native American women don't like it, but they were brought up to follow their family's traditions, and they either accept it or don't discuss it."

"Geez," Cat said, "what a drag."

The women were assigned the food and childcare duties; the men did the constructing, preparation for the drum, the dancing, and the ceremonies. While Cat was enthralled with the various pieces of costumes she saw people carrying, she was unimpressed with the assigned duties. A bit grudgingly, she helped out with the cooking.

Cheryl had brought a large cast iron pot and built a fire in the tepee. Then, she showed Cat where to get the water they would have to carry to the tepee for cooking and drinking. They carried pails of water so that Cheryl could fill the iron pot and put the beans in it to soak that she had brought for the feast. She was making black beans to add to the shared dinner, and she needed to make a lot as they expected over one hundred people. Cat had no idea there were so many people involved in powwows. After they got the pot in place over the fire, the water boiling and the beans cooking, Cheryl and Cat made their way to the area where the enclosed potties were lined up for the powwow. They were far enough away from the tepees so people couldn't smell them in the hot summer sun, but once you got near them, they stunk. Cat hated to use them, but it seemed the right thing to do. She hadn't even thought about such things—getting water, going to the bathroom, cooking over an open fire. It was a whole new world.

By early evening, everyone was carrying pots of food from their tepees to the long, plank tables. Sam carried the full cast iron pot for Cheryl. Some people had brought dried beef and added it to their dishes. Cooked corn and fry bread[15] were other offerings, along with honey and confectionary sugar to put on the fry bread. Cat had never even heard of fry bread. It was delicious. Some of the food was unidentifiable so Cat left it alone in favor of eating the things that looked like what she knew. Some pots were said to have bear meat in the stew and Cat definitely passed on those. Some people had made what looked like chicken, but since Cat wasn't sure, she stuck with the beans Cheryl had made, the corn and the fry bread. The meal was pretty heavy.

No alcohol was allowed at the powwow, so Cat drank tepid water served from a bucket. Then, it was time to dress for the dance. A large drum was encircled by a group of Native Americans sitting in folding chairs who seemed to be warming up. A fire pit that had been dug in the center and filled with stacked wood was lit. A young couple with a small child that they had met at the cooking area would stay with them, and share their tepee also. They had arrived in a car and needed a place to sleep. A couple who had hitchhiked there and knew Cheryl and Sam from other powwows also wanted to sleep in the tepee. Cat began to feel crowded and wondered how it would all work out. She went outside to sit on one of the benches arranged under the pine bough circle that enclosed the center, and defined the area for drumming and dancing.

Cheryl, Sam, and the newly arrived visitors were in the tepee dressing in their traditional dance costumes. Surrounded by tepees with poles that flew strips of fabric, rhythmic sounds of drumming, and the sounds of chanting and singing around the drum simply mesmerized Cat. She began to feel like she did when she had meditated with Ram Dass. She tucked herself against a bench out of the way, closed her eyes and let the sounds of the drum wash over her.

Rustling noises, sounds of bells and rattles brought her back. When other dancers came out of their tepees, it looked like an old photograph from another time. Traditional Native American costumes were everywhere. Some of the younger Native Americans were wearing the newer, bright-colored shirts and feathers, but the older costumes with earth colors and partridge feathers were beautiful. Cat had seen such things in museums, and here they were, coming to life. Also, the men danced in one direction and had the fancier costumes and dance steps, while the women danced in the other direction wearing dresses of deerskin and calico fabric with beautiful shawls. The beaded moccasins, Cheryl had told Cat, were often made by the wearer. Cheryl had beaded both her moccasins and Sam's, but Sam had made the pattern for them and had sewn the deerskin tops to the elk hide soles with sinew.

Cat sat on a bench and was soon transported on the sounds of the drum, the men's singing voices and the visual imagery as dancers made their way around the crackling fire. As time went on, children grew sleepy and were put to bed in their family's tepee, and then the parents could return because all the doors faced the dance area.

"What a great way to raise children," Cat said to Cheryl.

"Try living in one full-time," Cheryl said and went off with Sam to join the throngs of dancers.

The music carried Cat's thoughts upward to feelings of a connectedness that she yearned to be part of. Here was this community of people committed to upholding ancient traditions, something she knew was lacking today. Part of living with friends communally, she thought, was to connect, to share. Perhaps joining up with the American Indian Movement[16], known as AIM, would be a good idea. She had heard that representatives would be speaking at the powwow during the course of the weekend.

Dancing and drumming lasted deep into the night. Somehow, everyone slept in the tepee. Cat was too tired to worry about how many people there were and how close they were to each other. Early Sunday morning, the sound of the drum awoke Cat and she slipped outside before everyone else began to stir.

There, in the early morning light, sat Sam with a Native American man with his leather-tipped drumstick lightly making rhythmic sounds on the large drum. No one else appeared to be up yet so Cat sat on the ground to unobtrusively observe. The drummer had one feather attached to the back of his head, long silky black hair to his waist, and wore a breechcloth that showed off his strong thigh muscles. Cat guessed she was staring, because he cast a quick glance her way and she lowered her eyes. Soon, small children were out and about, mothers chasing them to go to the portable potties and telling them to wash up. Cook pots were on the fires and breakfast smells began to fill the air. Sam and the Native American man got up to leave. Sam returned to the tepee, smiled at Cat and went inside. The Native American man walked away between the farthest tepees from where Cat sat.

Later that morning, she recognized him as the man who spoke about the American Indian Movement, and the importance of donating to it. A blanket was carried around in the center circle and everyone threw dollars into it. Cat had a twenty-dollar bill that she dropped in when it went by. She noticed most of the bills were ones and fives. Midway during the prior evening, a blanket was also carried around to gather money. That donation was to support the people who had come from New Mexico and Arizona to play the drum for the powwow, and would help pay for their travel. She had thrown a twenty in then, too.

In retrospect, she wished she had carried smaller bills. She had stuffed a small purse full of twenty-dollar bills before leaving the commune in case she needed money, not knowing it would be donations that could be openly viewed. She hated feeling different or appearing to have money in the presence of those who might not, and felt some curious glances.

At the end of the day, they packed up their gear, and dismantled the tepee. Sam rolled it up, and placed it in the back of the truck bed before they took down the poles. They had to be lashed upon the wood bars over the truck so that each pole fit into place. Finally, it looked the same as when they had arrived the day before. They buried the center fire in ashes, then poured water over it, then replaced the piece of sod they had taken out. Cat found the whole idea romantic and mystical, oddly old and yet so new to her. She wished she could meet a Native American man who would show her their ways. Cheryl said that Sam had been studying ancient traditions for years. He was always invited to giveaways and presented with amazing gifts usually not given to whites. Cat looked at Sam with new eyes.

When they drove back, all were tired, thoughtful and quiet on the trip. Cat held the picture of the evening dance in her mind and she could hear the drum, the singing and sense of peace it gave her. Thoughts of the Native American man drumming with Sam played through the background images in her mind. She thought about watching him walk back to his tepee and imagined following him. *What would have happened if I had?* She wondered.

Cat was overtired Monday morning and couldn't go to work. She had convinced Eli to stay another day so they could go down to the lake together.

"Eli, you should come to the lake with me and sit under the umbrella. You could read and enjoy the breeze off the water, too."

"I suppose as the only black person for miles, it is my duty to raise the consciousness of this back woods town. All right, I will do it."

Nina had gone to work on time, and after Cat and Eli had coffee on the front porch, they got into their bathing suits and drove to the lake with towels, sun lotion and a beach umbrella. Cat had gotten quite a burn in her bikini last time, and while she enjoyed the healthy look a tan gave her, today she was going to sit under the umbrella, too.

Eli brought a Kurt Vonnegut paperback to read. Cat was still filled with thoughts about the powwow and wished she had a book to read about Native American traditions.

"Maybe on the way home, we can stop at the library in town," Cat said.

"Why?" asked Eli. "We have so many great books that everyone has brought to the commune."

"I really want to learn more about Native Americans. The powwow was pretty impressive, and I am still wondering about so much of it. I think it would be interesting to find out more historical information."

"Probably written by white men about a culture they could never understand and by the way—raped their women, killed their children, poisoned them with alcohol and drove into near extinction," said Eli.

"That was then, this is now," countered Cat. "We have to begin where we are now, Eli. Change happens when people learn from past mistakes, not repeat them!"

"You're such an idealist, Cat."

"Why, Eli? Why do you say that?"

Eli looked away and shook his head. "Your average white bread American doesn't think like you."

"That would be your average white male. Women are still second class citizens."

When they got to the lake, only some mothers with small children were there. Cat wondered about the reaction to Eli. As they got out of the Jeep, heads turned. They walked toward the end of the sandy beach area and Cat spread out two towels. She put the umbrella up in the sand, and Eli picked up a rock to drive the post down. Then, he took off his shorts, and folded them, placing them on the beach towel before sitting down. He was in a blue European bathing suit, skin tight, with a noticeably bulging front.

Some of the women gasped. One covered her daughter's eyes and walked away toward the other end of the beach.

Cat sat on her beach towel trying to be comfortable in the shade while Eli spread out to read his book, *Slaughterhouse-Five*. Cat knew that naming the commune Cat's Cradle must have been based on Vonnegut's book of the same name. They discussed some of the points regarding the Atomic bomb references in *Cat's Cradle*. Cat began to relax, and they talked about the way the otherworldly alien Tralfamadorians viewed life—as if each event was a bright, separate orb, like a bright spot of light—when the local police car pulled up.

Lost in conversation, until the crunch of boots on sand came in their direction, they didn't notice that Deputy Shepherd was approaching. Cat raised her head and then sat up straightening the straps on the top of her bikini. Eli glanced up through his sunglasses.

"Hello, Deputy Shepherd," Cat said.

"Hello, Mrs. Janson," he replied.

"Are you coming to the lake today?" Eli tried to sound innocent.

The deputy cleared his throat.

"I got a call from a lady in town that there was an offensive-looking bathing suit at the beach."

"Me?" asked Cat.

"No." He answered, glaring at Eli.

Picture yourself in a boat on a river,
With tangerine trees and marmalade skies
Somebody calls you, you answer quite slowly,
A girl with kaleidoscope eyes...

John Lennon, The Beatles,
"Lucy In The Sky With Diamonds," *Let It Be*, 1970

Chapter 12

Cheryl and Sam had moved into their summer tepee on the back of acres of land that belonged to Sam's family. An old farmhouse had burned down many years ago leaving behind the stones that were once part of its structure. A pile of stones formed a cellar hole, and they could use it to store some of the household items that wouldn't fit in the tepee by throwing a tarp over a partially enclosed area. When Nina ran into Cheryl at High Health, they had invited everyone on the commune to come for a potluck supper in August and enjoy the home they had made. The days were still warm, sometimes hot, but the nights were cool and less filled with mosquitoes than in July.

"Too bad the kids are away," Cat said to Nina.

"I know. They would just love it." Nina replied, as she had returned from visiting her former in-laws and left the boys to spend time with their grandparents and father.

During the summer with Lenora going back to Connecticut, only Cat, Nina and Davy remained. School was out for Davy until September and Eli came up weekends, arriving Friday nights and taking care of the calendar.

He would announce, "Eli's here!" upon his arrival, running with arms open wide, blowing kisses. He would pinch Davy's buttocks. Nina and Cat would roll their eyes at each other. Davy giggled, his silky blonde hair shaking, making him look even younger than his eighteen years. As soon as Cat told Eli about the potluck supper Saturday night at the tepee, he rummaged into a kitchen drawer for his red pen and wrote in the calendar, "Sam and Cheryl—Tipi Pot Luck."

They woke up in their own time Saturday morning, and over breakfast, decided to go to the local pond for a swim to cool down during the August heat wave they were having. Cat asked Eli twice about what bathing suit he was wearing.

"I know! I know!" an exasperated Eli replied. "I'm wearing the baggie shorts!"

They had found another pond off the main road with a little indentation that the Jeep fit into. The pond wasn't used by most people as it didn't have a sandy beach so Cat preferred this place to swim after her recent experience with Eli at the public beach.

"It must be 100 degrees," said Davy.

"At least," Nina replied. "I just hope it cools down tonight as we're supposed to cook over an open fire pit."

Davy and Eli grimaced.

"Oh, come on!" said Cat. "This will be fun. You should have seen all the tepees at the powwow. It was amazing." Cat turned over in the water and floated on her back.

"And would your life be incomplete if you didn't experience it again?" said Eli a bit loudly while dogpaddling to keep alongside Cat. "Wouldn't you rather barbeque on the porch and sip the wonderful margaritas I'll make in the blender. Cat, you did buy the ingredients I asked for?"

"Yes, yes, Eli, the limes, the special salt, the good tequila, all of it."

"Great, let's imbibe before heading into the wild. I wish I had brought my safari hat," Eli grumbled.

"For heaven's sakes! None of you would come to powwow with me, and now you're carrying on about visiting people who are our friends! It's important to keep our connections with others like us! We are the minority, in case you haven't noticed!"

"Who cares?" called Nina.

"Yeah, why do you care what other people think, Cat? Isn't that why we do our own thing? What other people think is their problem," said Davy.

"Here, here," said Eli. "I totally agree."

"Oh, fuck off!" said Cat.

They all soaked in the clear lake water long enough to feel cool and refreshed. In spite of the heat, and the words exchanged, the ride home wasn't so bad.

After they returned from the swim, Nina made a potato salad to bring. She hated to heat up the kitchen cooking the potatoes, but as soon as they were done, she ran them under the cold water in the sink and added ice cubes to the bowl.

Cat made a salad of fresh greens, tomatoes, celery, carrots, basil and black olives. She cut up onions to serve on the side and a simple dressing to bring.

Eli created designer hors d'oeuvres with little herbed mushrooms on toast points, which he made after removing the bread crust. He wanted something he could "chill and serve" so he wouldn't have to do anything with his hands but beat away the bugs.

Davy was shamed into doing something. His culinary skills were not yet evident so he grabbed a bunch of bananas and arranged them in a bowl. Then, he stood one up in the center.

"What's that?" asked Nina, pointing at the standing banana with a slightly annoyed look on her face.

"Look familiar?" asked Davy.

"Oh, brother!" Nina laughed, and then kissed Davy, hard. They looked at each other a moment and went upstairs.

Cat and Eli put together the containers in the kitchen and after awhile, Nina and Davy returned, grinning and holding hands.

Nina found the bug spray in the family room closet. They went outside to the yard and took turns spraying each other. Then, Eli made margaritas and they gathered on the front porch to sip them.

"Do you think Sam and Cheryl will know that we sprayed ourselves with this poisonous stuff?" asked Cat.

"Oh, please!" Nina said. "We're going there to eat, not to be eaten!"

"Well, that depends," said Davy.

"Oh, yeah!" said Eli.

"God! All you guys ever talk about is sex!" said Cat.

"You got that right!" laughed Davy. He took Nina's hand and pulled her inside.

"It's almost time to go," said Cat, annoyance in her voice and a scowl on her face.

"First we'll come, and then we'll go," said Davy.

Nina made a shrug, grinning, as her response to Cat, and they went upstairs again.

Eli hollered after them: "Be careful where you touch! That bug spray will mess you up!" He went into the kitchen and began to gather up the food.

Eli and Cat carried everything to the back of the Jeep and placed it in separate cardboard boxes hoping it wouldn't jump all over the place. First they had to make sure everything fit well, and then use dishtowels to secure the containers within the boxes. Finally, more plastic wrap was put over the tops. By the time they were loaded up, Nina and Davy came out of the house and got into the backseat in what Eli called "a post-coital smoothie" and curled up together.

Eli drove Cat's Jeep as she sat with a cranky expression on her face.

"Somebody's not getting any," Eli began.

"Oh stuff it, Eli," said Cat.

"I saw Tim in Connecticut. Remember Tim?"

"Yes," Cat said, looking out the open window.

"Well? Tim said he's written you letters and called you on the phone, and you haven't wanted him to come up to stay with you again."

"I feel badly, but he's only eighteen and—"

"You didn't mind a few months ago," said Eli.

"I know, I know, but it just seems—"

"Don't knock eighteen," Nina cut in. "They need very little sleep."

The Jeep swayed as they drove onto the old logging road that would lead to Cheryl and Sam's tepee.

"Whoa, Nellie," said Eli, as the old dirt road had not been graded, and deep ruts pulled the wheel out of his hands.

"Gee-eeez!" said Davy as he bounced in the backseat, hitting his head on the crossbar. Nina was leaning over the backseat holding onto the boxes to steady them.

"Watch it!" said Cat as Eli swerved around a stand of trees.

"I can see where I'm going," said Eli tersely. "Obviously, this isn't a road at all—unless we had a horse and buggy!"

The Jeep bumped along, tilting and jostling the occupants and food boxes for a good mile before coming to a grassy clearing. Finally, the land smoothed out for the last little bit of the journey.

"Well," said Eli, "if this is a hideout, they are certainly safe."

Nina laughed.

The tepee sat up on a hill at the end of the clearing. The simple structure of canvas and poles looked displaced, as if dropped there from another moment in time. The mountains were the backdrop in the distance, and everyone grew silent as they took it all in. Cat thought it looked beautiful standing alone.

Sam walked toward them from the woods to the left of the clearing. He was wearing a blue printed calico shirt Cheryl had sewn with long sleeves and ribbons across the chest. The color made his blue eyes stand out sharply. A bone necklace was wrapped closely around his neck like a choker and two shells were attached to his braids. A single feather stuck out of the back of his head. Cat noticed he was wearing some of the things he wore at the powwow.

"Leave the Jeep there," he commanded. "We like to keep the pollution at bay as much as possible."

"Sure," Eli said. "We have quite a bit to carry, though."

"No problem, we have a wheelbarrow."

"But, my hors d'oeuvres!" Eli protested.

"You can carry them," said Cat, smiling at Sam.

"Sam," Nina called out, "your shirt is beautiful but aren't you hot in it?"

"No, I was in the woods where the brook runs and it's pretty cool there. It's always cooler closer to the water and trees."

They all jumped out and unloaded the food into the wheelbarrow, which Sam steered toward the tepee. Cheryl held open the door flap. It was surprisingly cool inside. The smell of the earth and pine needles rose up from the ground. Sage smoldered on a stone adding to the pungent odors that met them. Braided sweet grass hung from a pole just inside the door flap.

"Welcome, everyone," Cheryl said, smiling. She was wearing a simple calico jumper that had tiny blue and green flowers on it.

"Nice to see you again, Cheryl," Cat said. Her jeans and t-shirt didn't feel all that cool. She hadn't spoken to Cheryl or Sam since the powwow and wanted to be sure and tell them how much she had appreciated them taking her. They each brought their dishes in the cardboard boxes into the tepee, and sat in a circle around the small fire. Sam sat at the head of the circle with Cheryl. Behind them was a bed with a buffalo throw. They had received the buffalo robe at a giveaway[17] at one of the recent powwows they had attended. While Cat was a little familiar with some of the tepee arrangements and items, everyone else was quite awestruck by the unusual artifacts.

Nina and Davy were "oohing" and "aahing" as they studied various hanging items.

Sam took a black stone pipe with a 30" long pipe stem out of a leather bag. He had recently completed weaving the porcupine quills to decorate the stem. Everyone admired the fine work as it was passed around. He also showed them a stone bowl that he had carved that was smooth and red. "This is catlanite," Sam instructed, "and it is only for sacred ceremony with tobacco." He put it back into the bag. Then Sam filled the black stone pipe bowl with something from a leather pouch and lit it. He handed it to Cat first.

When Cat took the pipe to smoke, she asked what the bowl was made of.

"I carved it out of soapstone," said Sam. "It's not sacred to the Native Americans." He smiled so Cat thought it must be some kind of pot in the bowl.

"Oh," Cat said. She took a toke and passed it on, holding the smoke in her lungs. Then she coughed at the sharpness.

"What's this?" Cat asked. It didn't taste like the hashish she had had before. This seemed much stronger.

"It's hashish," said Sam.

"Great stuff," said Davy.

"Delish," said Nina.

"Yum" said Eli. "We used to get it from Eddie and Amy once in awhile, but we haven't heard from them lately."

"I hope they're all right," said Nina, thinking of all of their travel and drug deals that could have turned dangerous.

Nina, Davy and Eli were becoming more comfortable with each passing of the pipe. Eli asked Sam about the hashish.

"Haven't seen any hash around for awhile," Eli said. "How did you get hold of it?"

"I have a connection through Gene," Sam said.

"Really?" asked Eli. "He never mentioned it when he came to visit and smoke up whatever Eddie and Amy brought from Boston."

"You know Scott, Gene's cousin—he's been crashing with them and has a lot of connections."

Cat glanced at Nina, but she was interested in other things.

Nina asked Sam about the bones and other items hanging in the tepee. Sam was explaining various meanings of the objects to her when Nina also noticed the moccasins both Sam and Cheryl wore. They were the same ones Cat had seen them wear at powwow.

"Sam made the moccasins and I did the beadwork," said Cheryl.

"Beautiful!" said Nina. "Is the beadwork hard to do?"

"No, it just takes a while to learn it and it's very slow going, but you get faster as time goes on."

Cat noticed small beaded pouches hanging from the tepee poles and more pipe stems that looked like quill work. She asked Cheryl about the stems.

"Those are quills that are woven so closely together that they look like beads. Sam does all the quill work," said Cheryl proudly. "I think it's harder than working with the beads."

"Wow." Cat hadn't seen all of their beadwork and pouches at the powwow. Cheryl took down another quilled pipe stem and passed it to Cat to see more closely. The quills were tightly woven and had been died deep colors which made each tiny section look similar to beads from a distance.

A small spinning wheel stood raised off the ground on a wooden palette pushed to the side of the bed.

"Do you spin wool, too?" Cat asked Cheryl.

"Oh, yes. I also dye the yarn with natural colors from herbs and vegetables." Cheryl turned around to point at some warm, light golden brown yarn hanging over the spinning wheel.

"See that color? That's from boiling onion skins."

"It is?" said Cat. "That's amazing!"

"Well, if you knew all the chemicals in dye, you wouldn't wear half the clothes that are out there. We also buy a lot of plain muslin and dye it ourselves. We want to be as self-sufficient as possible."

Cat was thinking about all this when Sam suggested they move outside to the table and benches that were set up behind the tepee.

They all got to their knees, and then slowly stood up with the full effects of hashish on top of margaritas and empty stomachs. As soon as the dishes of food were placed on the table, Eli swept up his tray of hors d'oeuvres and passed them to everyone.

They were inhaled in a matter of minutes.

A long, cast iron grille sat upon rocks that surrounded a fire pit. The coals had burned down enough to start cooking.

"We wrapped corn in foil and it's in the fire," said Cheryl, "and I brought hamburgers over from my mother's freezer. I think they're almost thawed out."

Cat wondered how tinfoil and frozen meat fit in with self-sufficiency and natural dyes.

"Good thing Lenora isn't here," Eli said under his breath, referring to the meat.

Nina, never one to let anything slide by, said, "How does tinfoil and frozen meat fit with living in a tepee and being self-sufficient?"

"It doesn't," laughed Cheryl. "We don't have it all figured out yet."

"We're moving toward it," said Sam, chuckling good-naturedly. "There are some things we can implement easily enough but I haven't figured out how to dry meat yet and store all our food."

They all grinned.

Sam walked over to the nearby brook that flowed from the mountain and along the entry into the woods beyond them, and pulled out two six-packs of beer bottles. He snapped off the tops with his Swiss army knife and passed them out. After smoking the hash, everyone drank thirstily. Cat and Nina got the salads ready.

"Here—have some salads to start," Nina said, so they could fill their paper plates and start eating while waiting for the burgers to cook. With long fire tongs, Cheryl poked through the coals and pulled out the corn. Some of it was charred around the edges, but it tasted just right with the salad. They all sat along the benches eating in silence while listening to the buzzing of the insects. The citron candles Sam had put around the table in cups helped a bit in keeping away the mosquitoes, but both Sam and Cheryl confided that dealing with mosquitoes and no-see-ums was their biggest challenge so far.

"The Native Americans used bear grease to keep from being bitten," Sam began.

"Bear grease?" asked Cat. "Sounds terrible."

"And smells awful!" offered Cheryl.

They all laughed.

"We also found lemon-scented body oil from the health food store that seems to help," said Sam.

"But it's expensive," added Cheryl. "And we can't use food stamps to buy it."

"Food stamps?" asked Cat.

"Yes, since Sam was laid off at the mill and the nearby diner closed, neither of us has worked since last winter."

"Oh." Cat nodded but she didn't know of anyone who had ever had food stamps. She thought they were for the very poor. She supposed if you didn't have any income—or a job—you could get very poor very fast. She had not thought about that before. Throughout the months of her separation, bits of money had come from her family, and she and her husband split the costs of the farm except the groceries and shared items with Nina, Davy, Eli and Lenora. Like pot, and hash, for example. The idea of being poor enough to need food stamps was a new and frightening thought.

Sam checked the hamburgers and Cat and Eli exchanged glances. She knew he would chime in later about that conversation. He always said she should watch out that she didn't become like that Bob Dylan song, "How does it feel, to be on your own, with no direction Home, like a complete unknown, like a rolling stone..."

As the sun began to set, they feasted on the smoky-tasting hamburgers while watching the colors change over the mountains.

"Red sky at night, sailor's delight," Cat called out.

"Red sky in the morning, sailor take warning." answered Nina.

"Growing up near sailboats," Cat added to answer the quizzical looks they received. "Both Nina and I grew up outside of Boston near the ocean, and spent a lot of time walking around the boating docks in the summer. We used to have friends who would dive for lobsters, and then we would cook them at the beach in a fire pit that we dug in the sand. Being outdoors with a fire sure recalls a lot of memories."

"That's true, Cat. I remember when things like divorce weren't even in my thoughts."

"So do I, so do I," said Cat shaking her head slowly side-to-side.

As if to change the somberness of the moment, Sam said, "I sure feel mellow—anything in those mushrooms, Eli?"

"They were sautéed and lightly herbed for stuffing," Eli answered. "Been a good while since I had any real 'shrooms."

Everyone laughed, except Cat who didn't get the joke.

"You know," Sam continued, "I have a fair amount of 'silly' mushrooms."

"Really?" said Nina, Davy and Eli all together.

"What's in them?" asked Cat.

All eyes turned to her.

"Ho, ho," said Eli. "A virgin!" and clapped his hands together.

"It's psilocybin, a hallucinogenic," said Sam.

Cheryl laughed. "We call it 'silly-siben.' I'll go get them."

Cat felt uncomfortable. She didn't want to take them.

Eli turned to Cat and began to explain to her that they wouldn't be a big deal. They weren't much different than hashish.

When Cheryl passed them each an equal amount to take, Cat wanted to refuse but said, "I don't know. Maybe not this time."

"Do a little less," said Cheryl. "I've tried these and it's been a pretty cool experience, not scary at all."

"Far out," said Davy. "I'll eat any Cat doesn't want."

"That's okay," said Cheryl. "We should set a few aside in case Cat doesn't get off. They affect everyone differently."

Cat took half the mushrooms Cheryl offered and waited to watch how everyone would take them.

Sam got another six-pack of beer for them to swallow the mushrooms with.

"They taste awful. Just chew them up a bit and then wash them down with the beer," he instructed.

Nina said it was time for Davy's dessert once they finished the mushrooms. Davy uncovered the bowl of bananas only to be met with the fact that they had all turned brown. "Yuk, what happened here?" Nina asked.

"Looks like you didn't squeeze lemon juice on them," said Eli. "That might have slowed down the browning process."

"We can give them to the ant people," said Cheryl, smiling. She took a large skillet off the side of the fire pit. She had made bread in it and put it on the table with a plastic bottle of honey that reminded Cat of the powwow's fry bread.

Cheryl read her thoughts, "It's not fry bread, Cat. I haven't learned how to make it yet without getting burned."

After awhile, Cat felt a bit queasy and she noticed her vision seemed different. She felt as if she were either ahead or behind her movements. As she was trying to decide which it was, everyone returned to sit around the table, sipping their beer and picking at the bread and drizzling honey on it. They grew silent. After what seemed like a long time, Cat realized she had to pee. "Do you have an outhouse?" Laughter came to her from far away. She looked around but it seemed to be everyone at the table laughing. The sound seemed to roll toward her from the distance.

Sam smiled. "We have to use the woods but I'll show you where to go."

As Cat followed Sam across the clearing, she felt disconnected from her motions. At times, she felt like her feet were drifting over the grass. She laughed to herself, and then wondered if she had laughed out loud or silently.

Sam held back some tree limbs that hung over the path. "Go ahead," he pointed.

"It's dark," Cat said.

"Your eyes will adjust," said Sam.

"I can't see anything."

"Follow the line of the brook," said Sam patiently. "Then go to the left, the path veers to the left."

"You go first," said Cat.

"All right." said Sam, he flashed a grin at Cat and walked in front of her.

As he walked ahead of her, he pointed to the brook to help Cat see where she was. Cat saw the shimmer of the water and got a bit lost in it. When she looked up, Sam was nowhere around. She just stood there for a while. Then she moved toward the pitch-black woods.

"Sam?"

"Over here," Sam said.

"Where are you?"

"Follow the sound of my voice."

Cat stumbled along, tripping over roots and low bushes, then to where she could just make out the side of Sam. He was peeing.

"Just there is fine," he said, pointing to an area a few feet away from him.

Cat dropped her pants and peed. She felt relieved, and then realized she had nothing to wipe herself with.

"Toilet tissue?"

"You can use leaves, or you can drip dry, you know." Sam said and chuckled.

Cat felt around for leaves, hoping it wasn't anything buggy. Sam noticed her confusion rustling around on the ground and picked up some leaves nearby which he handed to her.

"Thanks, Sam."

"Sure."

He waited for her, and she followed him back to the brook. Cat knelt down and washed her hands.

Sam knelt down beside her and swished his hands in the water, too. "Nice and cold," Sam commented.

"Yes," Cat said. Through the all-encompassing darkness, little lights were in the water. She tried to catch them with her hands, and when she couldn't, began to touch the surface where she thought the lights would be next.

She was feeling her fingers play with the water, when she felt a rush of cold on her breasts. Sam was kneeling behind her with his cold, wet hands on her breasts, and he began gently squeezing her startled nipples. He kissed the back of her neck.

"What—" Cat began.

"Shh," Sam said, and pressed his body to hers knocking her off balance. She fell back onto him and they rolled over on the ground. They both laughed.

At the table, each person floated in his or her experience, feeling sensations from the psilocybin. Eli chewed on a piece of bread and stared at the stars. You could see so many stars in the country sky at night. He wanted to lie on the ground on his back like a little kid and stare at all the twinkles, maybe see a comet.

Nina was carving a piece of bread into the shape of a penis. She almost had it right, too, when Davy put his hand on hers. It felt like an electric current went through her. She turned to look at him. Cheryl noticed them and laughed softly, enjoying the slowed motion. "I feel like I am inside a soap bubble," she announced to no one in particular, then laughed and laughed until it turned into giggles.

Her laughter spread, and soon everyone was laughing and enjoying the shared moment.

As they quieted down, Davy slid his hand under Nina's shirt and began to rub one of her breasts. Nina continued carving the bread. Cheryl began to build a stack of bread pieces and poured honey over it like pancakes. Eli drifted back to childhood memories at his first summer camp when he could see all the stars in the sky for the first time. Nina felt herself growing warm from Davy's touch and almost cut her finger on the knife. She pushed Davy's hand away. Cheryl's stack of bread toppled over.

Davy said to Nina, "Come on."

"Later," Nina said.

"Don't stop on my account," laughed Cheryl.

Then, she looked toward the woods. "Where's Sam and Cat?"

Sam rolled over on top of Cat and kissed her full on the mouth. He pressed his body against hers and spread her legs with his legs. He lifted her shirt and stroked her breasts and began to lick her nipples with his tongue.

Cat let out a low moan. Surprised, stoned from the hash and drifting into new sensations from the mushrooms, she wasn't sure if she was really doing what she might be doing.

Sam unfastened the top button of her jeans and unzipped the fly, pulling the legs of her jeans down. Then, he undid his own jeans, and pushed them down while sliding on top of her. She was aware of the pine needles beneath her, and prickly objects were sticking into her back and buttocks. But then, Sam put his fingers in his mouth, moistened them, and slid them between her legs.

"Ohhhh," she moaned with pleasure as Sam moved himself into position and entered her. He rocked her gently, and held her tightly to him. She felt deeply aroused with every thrust, and waves of pleasure filled her. At the same time, she wanted to say something about her discomfort, and began to speak with her eyes closed tight, trying to keep the thought from slipping away.

"Ohh, ohhh, Sam, things are sticking into me," Cat began.

A disembodied voice said, "I'll bet they are."

As Cat opened her eyes, she saw Cheryl standing over them.

FALL 1975

...You can get it if you really want
You can get it if you really want
But you must try, try and try
Try and try, you'll succeed at last...

Jimmy Cliff,
"You Can Get It If You Really Want,"
The Harder They Come soundtrack, 1972

Chapter 13

The children had returned to the commune after the summer. Nina and Cat had driven south to meet the respective fathers at the same place—a rest area north of the city with a coffee shop. When Cat saw Laura and Becky, she had to work to keep from crying, and Nina's eyes were shiny when Erin and Nathan got out of their father's car. Laura and Becky ran over to Erin and Nathan first, clearly pleased to see each other, before noticing their mothers.

All of the children looked out of the Jeep windows to wave at their fathers as they pulled out of the parking area. Cat felt filled with emotion and had to concentrate on driving.

Nina began to tell the kids stories about the garden, and what vegetables were growing that they could eat. She said that the summer was quiet without them, and began to steer the conversation toward asking them about their summer. Cat couldn't speak as she felt her voice would betray her swirling emotions.

After awhile, the children began to talk, and soon everyone was chatting again like they had before they left. They talked animatedly to each other about their camp experiences, and the new friends they had made. Nina and Cat exchanged glances. Holding each other's eyes, they both took a deep breath, exhaling long and slow.

When they drove into the side yard, Laura, Becky, Erin and Nathan couldn't wait to jump out of the Jeep and run into the house. By now, Nina and Cat were beginning to feel better about their children's return. It was always a bit strained whenever they returned from their fathers.

"They seem fine, don't you think?" asked Nina.

"Yeah, I do, and I think the kids having each other has helped."

Eli had a flyer that he picked up at the High Health Cooperative. An outside music festival was being held this very weekend with lots of people in the area, many of whom lived on farms, in communes, and some who wanted to start an intentional community. This would celebrate the end of summer and the beginning of the school year for the children. Since it began in the morning, there were games planned like three-legged races, and an egg and spoon toss. Everyone thought it was the perfect way to end the summer. Davy was still in school and was in Cambridge each week, but Eli was back to stay. Lenora had found a job in Cambridge, and was living with Davy and Jimmy during the week. She drove up with Davy some weekends.

So they took the Datsun and the Jeep. Davy, Nina and the boys went in the Datsun, and Eli, Cat and the girls drove in the Jeep. Rather than have a potluck, it had been catered by those who raised their own food. Everyone paid five dollars—*more than fair*, thought Cat. It was so rare that she didn't have to make something everywhere they went. She frankly enjoyed the freedom.

Quite a few people sought out Eli and engaged him in conversation. If Cat wasn't wrong, there seemed to be a line up of people who wanted to get to know him. Some thought he had been in the theater, but hadn't seen him in any of the plays. Eli ate up the attention and had worn a bit of eye makeup for the occasion. Cat no longer noticed.

The day passed beautifully, everyone busy, the children seeing friends from school who, they discovered, lived in communal households like they did. Jessica, Gene and his cousin Scott were there, as were Pam and Brad. Sam and Cheryl came by for a while, and all seemed forgiven from the incident of Cheryl finding Sam and Cat in the woods. Cat was a little apprehensive when she first saw them walking toward her, but felt comfortable talking to them. The sounds of live bands playing outside in the breezy afternoon, the adults sipping beer and passing joints around, and the children happily involved in games and activities added to Cat's sense of well-being.

Finally, Eli was free to walk over to Cat.

"Isn't this great? What a super day!" said Cat.

"I know! Half of the people here have either worked at High Health or shop there! It's like we have all seen each other before!" said Eli.

"I didn't know so many other children lived in communes, either," said Cat. "I hope this makes the kids feel comfortable when they start the school year."

Nina and Davy came over to them to share a joint. The band began playing some really good rock 'n' roll and they all started to dance. The day seemed to go on and on. None of them suspected that this would be one of the last fun gatherings before everything would begin to change.

That evening, Eli wanted to go to a local place in town where one of the bands they enjoyed that day was going to play. He had met and talked with the guys in the band, and he was sure one of them liked him. Cat wanted to go because she had noticed one of the guys in the band, too, and he seemed to be checking her out when she was dancing with Eli. Although they were at a distance, he was tall with straight, black hair and looked like a Native American. He wore his hair loose, like the dancers at powwow, and Cat found him terribly attractive. Nina and Davy offered to bathe and put the children to bed so that Cat could go.

As they left, Nina called out, "Have at it, girlfriend! Been a long time since you got laid!" *Not counting the indiscretion with Sam*, she supposed.

They arrived after the band had started playing and there were no more seats near the front. They found two chairs, but no table, along the side of the wall by the speakers. Eli insisted they sit there. Cat asked someone nearby for two cigarettes, broke off the filters, and stuck them in her ears.

When she looked over at the band, the man she was interested in was looking at her. She felt a zinging sensation from meeting his gaze and flushed to her hair roots. Then she looked away. Several more times, she would sneak a peek at him and he would always know it. Then she remembered—she had seen him at powwow! She was sure of it! That must be why he noticed her!

Soon, Sam and Cheryl showed up with Gene, Jessica and Scott. They pulled some chairs over close to Eli and Cat, and when the band stopped playing, Cat asked Sam and Cheryl, "Is that guy in the band the drummer I saw at powwow with you last summer?"

"No," said Sam, looking annoyed. "All Native Americans don't look alike."

Cat felt chastised. It was an honest mistake. She looked away.

Cheryl looked at Sam and then at Cat. She didn't say anything.

When the band took a break, the band members came over to the table. The man who reminded Cat of the handsome Native American from powwow walked right over to Sam and shook his hand.

"Haven't seen you since the powwow, white brother," he said, looking a bit mischievous.

Sam smiled sheepishly and stood up. "Hello, Deer Horn, how are you?"

"Well, very well. Hello, Cheryl."

"Ya-ta-hey, Deer Horn."

I would be even better if you would introduce me to this lovely lady," he said looking at Cat.

"Deer Horn, this is Cat from Cat's Cradle Commune, that farm on the hill I told you about?"

"How do you do, Cat." Deer Horn stared deep into her eyes, smiling.

Cat shivered, held out her hand, and said, "F-f-fine, thank you."

When his hand touched hers, she felt a surge of energy run through her body. Deer Horn chuckled. "I saw you at powwow with Sam and Cheryl. I would like to see your commune."

Cat could barely think. When the band returned to finish the set, she turned to Eli for support. Eli smiled at her. "You may have got lucky," he said.

"I don't know if I want to be 'lucky,'" Cat replied.

Sam turned toward her. "Be careful," he admonished. "Deer Horn is powerful medicine."

"Oh, honestly, Sam," Cheryl said. "Give it a rest." Cheryl continued, "I went out with Deer Horn when I first went to powwow a couple of years ago."

"And you slept with him," Sam stated.

"Well, of course I did!" Cheryl answered.

The table was quiet amid the thundering music as it built up to a drum solo by Deer Horn himself. Cat was glad she had put the filters in her ears, but didn't think they made much difference.

When it was over, past midnight, Deer Horn boldly came over and sat down next to Cat. "Well?" he asked.

"Well, what?" Cat replied.

"Can I go home with you and see your commune?"

Cat began, "I have children, and—"

"That's nice. I would still like to go home with you." He ran his hand down the length of her arm. Cat felt goose bumps rise, and heat between her legs all at the same time. His eyes held hers, and she felt like she would tip over backwards if she wasn't careful.

"All right," she said.

When they all rose to leave, Sam was scowling and picking at something on his sleeve.

"A penny for your thoughts," Cheryl said to him under her breath.

Deer Horn spoke to the members of the band. They all wanted to go to the commune. Deer Horn said their van would follow her home. Eli said, "I have a better idea, you drive with Cat and I'll drive with the band."

Before Cat could say anything, Deer Horn said, "Great."

In the parking lot, Deer Horn offered to drive the Jeep.

Cat was so shaky, she didn't know if she could drive anyway, so she handed him her keys. The long, winding dirt road steadily climbed, and the van was somewhat behind them as it was filled with people and equipment.

As they crested the hill toward the farm, Cat turned to Deer Horn, "Kiss me. Kiss me now."

He pushed in the clutch, stepped on the break, and grabbed her close, kissing her hungrily. Cat's head was spinning.

A horn beeped behind them, he released her, and said, "The van caught up to us!"

When they parked in the side yard, Cat led them all into the family room. She thought it would make less noise then going through the house.

After checking on her daughters, Cat showed the band where the kitchen was and the downstairs bathroom. The guys in the band could sleep in the family room on the sofas. Eli had gone off to be alone as he discovered they were all straight. The guys asked if she had any beer and she quickly provided it for them. They sat around playing with a couple of their guitars. Cat and Deer Horn went up into the loft.

"I noticed you at, powwow," Cat began.

"And I noticed you, too, Cat."

Cat smiled and felt a bit shy. She was also aware of the band members in the room below, practicing chords, adjusting strings on their guitars, and the clink of beer bottles. Deer Horn took her hand and led her to the bed at the back of the loft.

"Your hair is beautiful," said Cat.

"So is yours," said Deer Horn, smiling, as he held a strand of her blonde hair next to his shiny, black hair.

Deer Horn turned Cat to face him. "Let's lie down and just look into each other's eyes."

Cat thought, I bet he used that line before. It works.

A couple of the musicians were smoking joints. The sounds of strumming, the smell of marijuana, and the low conversation began to lull Cat into the feeling of being far away.

Cat felt mesmerized by Deer Horn's focused attention, and as she stared into his eyes, she felt like she was slipping into a deep, dark pool.

They held each other gently and Deer Horn began stroking her shoulders, her arms, and her breasts. As they kissed, she wrapped herself around him, drinking him in. His warmth and soft touches made her feel excited, yet peaceful at the same time. They undressed each other very slowly, savoring the moment. Later, they fell asleep entwined in each other's arms.

When she awoke early the next morning, Deer Horn and the band were gone.

It is the evening of the day
I sit and watch the children play
Smiling faces I can see
But not for me...

Mick Jagger and Keith Richards, The Rolling Stones,
"As Tears Go By", *December's Children*, 1965

Chapter 14

The local real estate agency called Cat one Saturday to say that a "nice" couple from New York had driven past the farm and wanted to see it on Sunday. Cat was taken aback. She knew as part of the divorce settlement, her husband had said they would have to sell the farmhouse, but she hadn't realized it was already listed. It had seemed like a distant idea whose time would come—when Cat was ready. As soon as she got off the telephone, she went around the house looking at the bedrooms and the family room, and fretting about how long it would take to make everything look cleaned up by 2:00 p.m. Sunday afternoon.

"Nina, the Realtor called and said they want to show the house tomorrow! We have so much to do!" Cat wailed.

"Leave everything the way it is, then maybe they won't want to buy it," offered Nina.

"No, no! What if the Realtors talk to Daniel's lawyers? What if they say they saw marijuana here—or hash pipes? I can't take that chance!"

"Oh, come on Cat, it's practically legal!" said Lenora.

"No, no it isn't. It could be used in court against me. No," Cat said again.

It was a quiet weekend with just Lenora, Cat, Nina and their children. It wouldn't be too hard to orchestrate the clean up if everyone cooperated.

"You know, maybe it is time the farm was sold," Cat said, feeling aggravated by their blasé attitudes. "If anything happens, it doesn't affect you guys, it affects me."

Lenora and Nina exchanged glances and went off to their bedrooms to straighten things up a bit. Cat spoke to the children about helping by cleaning up their rooms, picking up their toys and clothes, and then she would give them ice cream. They all scampered off to do their chores.

That evening, Nina and Lenora were smoking joints in the family room right after dinner, not waiting for the children to be put to bed. Cat felt put out about their attitudes, and she felt they were trying to make this more difficult than it already was. She leaned into the family room before the children went in and called, "Hey, there's a full moon tonight. Want to drive up to the top of Mount Kenney to show the kids?"

"Naww," said Nina.

Lenora said. "Rather hang out and listen to music."

"Okay," Cat said brightly, "I'll drive them up there. I want to see it."

Cat told the four children about the adventure, they all ran out the front door, and piled into the Jeep to head up to the mountain. When they got to the top, other families were there with their children, sitting on blankets, sipping lemonade. Cat wished she had thought to bring blankets at least. The kids wore jackets, but the ground would be too cold to sit on. They walked for awhile beside an open area and there were some empty picnic tables.

"Hey, come on, let's sit here," Cat said.

Laura and Erin were talking about school. Laura was in second grade with Erin, so they had a lot to share. Becky and Nathan were in kindergarten in the next town, and they brought home brightly colored papers and printed pages of letters for Cat and Nina to hang all over the kitchen. They were laughing together and chasing each other in circles. Cat looked at them and thought it was a good thing they had each other as part of their extended family, and got along most of the time.

As the moon rose full, it seemed so close and so golden; everyone silently gazed at it. The top of the mountain was as light as day. Cat could see one of the teachers from school with her husband. Some of the kids on the mountain her children used to play with—until they weren't allowed to visit anymore. After talk of the farm turning into a commune, none of the local children were allowed to visit there. The four upturned faces were so innocent. Cat wondered how much effect living an alternative lifestyle was having on them. Had she done anything useful for her daughters? She thought she was more concerned about the quality of their lives than Nina was about her two sons. Perhaps it was, as Lenora said, her own nitpicking personality, her need to prove something. Everyone was always telling Cat to relax. Nina didn't think marijuana was a big deal, as long as there were no other drugs, except hash. Hash was okay.

Soon, it was time to walk back to the Jeep with the four children in tow. She held Becky's hand while Laura walked with Erin and Nathan ahead of them.

Sunday morning, Cat set her alarm for 7:00 a.m., got up to put on the coffee, and begin preparations for a proper breakfast for everyone. She pulled out the vacuum to clean the family room. When she went in, there wasn't a rolling paper or pipe or ashtray anywhere. Everything was clean as a whistle and appeared to have been vacuumed already. Pleasantly surprised, she went back into the kitchen to pour a cup of coffee and wait for everyone else to get up.

At 1:00 p.m., Lenora and Nina decided it would probably be best if they went to town with the boys. Cat said she'd keep the girls home even though they wanted to go with everyone to town. The fact was she didn't want to be alone with the real estate agent showing the house to some strangers. She had actually hoped everyone would stay with her.

"There's a bunch of hippies living at the old farm now," said the Realtor, Brian Denner, to the family who wanted to see the delightful-looking house and barn.

"Fine with us," laughed the man.

"It used to be in pristine condition before it was taken over by this couple from Boston, then they let all these people move in."

"That's okay," he said. "We've lived with friends in an old farmhouse ourselves." Brian was disappointed. He had hoped to regale them with tales of hippie behavior that he had heard about from the townspeople.

At almost 2:00 p.m., he pulled up and parked in front of the house. The agent got out of the car, followed by a couple with two daughters, and approached the front door where Cat waited. She opened it and greeted them amiably, then introduced her daughters to theirs. The girls asked them if they wanted to play in the family room. Cat led the procession through the house to the family room where the toy boxes were neatly lined up.

"Can we take the toys out now?" asked Becky.

Cat smiled. "Yes, now you can!"

She liked the couple she met, and wondered what her life would be like if she were still living with Daniel. *Would we all become friends?* She wondered. *Would we move to a house in town or back to Boston?* She couldn't see what the future would hold outside of her struggle to get custody of her children. She returned to the family room to be with them, and let the couple walk through the farmhouse by themselves with the Realtor.

...Oh, I get by with a little help from my friends
Mm, I get high with a little help from my friends
Mm, gonna try with a little help from my friends...

John Lennon and Paul McCartney, The Beatles,
"A Little Help From My Friends," as performed by
Joe Cocker, *Woodstock,* 1969

Chapter 15

Cat didn't know whether to laugh or cry.

Brian Denner called her the next day. "Good news! The people who visited you on Sunday have made an offer—they are willing to pay the asking price!"

"Oh, really? So soon?"

"Yup. They filled out the paperwork and Daniel's attorneys already approved it."

Cat knew Daniel couldn't wait to have her move out of what had become known as the town's only commune. *Probably, because it looks like a commune. Okay. It is a commune.* She had just hoped it wouldn't happen so soon.

The couple from New York was ready to pay cash. A simple closing could take place, but there was one catch—

they wanted to move in by Christmas. *Christmas! Where will I go?* thought Cat.

As soon as she got off the phone with the Realtor, she called Attorney Farley and told him there was an offer on the house. One of Daniel's attorneys had already called him.

"His attorneys keep putting off the depositions but say they want the house sold. No doubt it's because of all the people living there. You know, Daniel's attorneys say it's a commune."

Catherine couldn't say anything about that. "Yeah, but I don't know where to go."

"Well, it will give you some cash and let you start planning your own future, as long as you don't leave the state. We could petition to slow it down, but right now, you have a ready buyer."

"All right, I guess I will have to figure something out."

"Catherine?"

"Yes."

"Stop worrying! This will turn around right!"

"I wish I could believe that."

"It will! I mean it."

When she got off the phone, Cat told Nina and Lenora that after Thanksgiving, they would all have to move out. It was the only way she would have time to settle everything with Daniel, figure out where she was going to live, and if the children would have to change schools. Suddenly it was real. Her time at her beloved farmhouse was over. Cat couldn't go back to Boston even if she wanted to, but she didn't know what she was going to do.

First, she needed to get everyone's possessions out of the house and barn.

Nina got to work making phone calls to find out about any nearby rentals. She still had stacks of unopened boxes in the barn which would make moving easy enough. She hadn't needed a lot of things when she moved in barely a year ago. Now she was glad she hadn't unpacked.

Lenora wondered about her future. She could go back to school, or keep her job and stay in Cambridge, but, she did like coming to Vermont weekends.

After the calls were made, things began to develop quickly. Nina and her two boys were invited to move in with Jessica and Gene for the rest of the school year in their large, albeit unfinished, log cabin. Davy would still be in Cambridge at school so it seemed preferable for Nina to stay in Vermont with Erin and Nathan. Lenora could go back to Connecticut with Eli, who had finally decided to return to school. Lenora needed to think about it. Everyone's plans were taking shape although moving would be made more difficult with all the snow.

Jessica and Gene still had a few things in the barn and Nina passed on the fact that their boxes—and hers—would have to be removed from the barn.

Sam and Cheryl had been storing their tepee in the barn after moving into their winter home, and some trunks that held a lot of their dancing clothes and feathers for summer powwows. Cat thought she had better drive out of town to where they were staying and tell them, too.

The girls would be going to their father's for Thanksgiving week, which would give Cat time to clean up some of the loose ends. Daniel offered to keep them for December as well. Cat didn't like them to miss school, or be away from her that long, but it did seem like a practical idea. She would have to decide and call him during Thanksgiving weekend.

"Let's have a good-bye open house for Thanksgiving and invite all our friends," said Cat.

"That might be fun," said Nina as she carried another box to the family room.

"Not really, having a Thanksgiving holiday when we took this country away from its native people," began Lenora "is like celebrating the holocaust."

Cat cut in, "Well, that's pretty extreme, Lenora." She had learned how to fend off Lenora's constant critiques and put downs. "Hey, I've been looking at all the holiday recipes in the Woman's Day magazine—"

"What?" said Lenora. "You paid for that misogynist crap?"

"It has some great ideas for Thanksgiving! Every mainstream woman's magazine isn't misogynist, Lenora! Look, you hollow out a pumpkin, make soup and serve it right out of the pumpkin shell! Isn't that cool?" said Cat.

Lenora just smirked and looked away.

"Eli can help cook if he doesn't go to Connecticut, and we can get a huge turkey, and have a feast laid out on the dining room table," Cat continued ignoring Lenora.

"I think I'll be going to Connecticut by then," said Lenora.

Nina came back into the kitchen. "I think a holiday open house would be great. I can finish moving into Gene and Jessica's house and we can have them here for our last Thanksgiving. That would be fun!"

"Whoop-de-doo," said Lenora, rolling her eyes.

Nina and Cat sat down together to make phone calls and write down a shopping list on a piece of paper.

They invited Gene and Jessica with Scott—who was still messing around with seedlings in the barn and grow lights. Eddie and Amy would drive up with Davy after he finished his last class for the holiday break. Pam and Brad were going to her parents so they were out. Nina ticked off the people on her fingers: At the house it would be Cat, Davy, maybe Davy's housemate, Jimmy, Eddie, Amy, Eli, and maybe Lenora. Sam and Cheryl might come, and Cat would drive out there to invite them. Gene and Jessica and Scott would come, and perhaps a few more. If they planned for 15 to 20, they would be more than covered.

Lenora decided, begrudgingly, to stay and help out after all. She said that she would wash out the old fridge in the barn so they could store extra food and the piecrusts Eli would make. This would let them prepare some things ahead of time. Lenora liked physical work more than cooking anyway. It didn't take her long to pack her things, as she hadn't brought much to the farm to begin with. She packed up her macramé supplies that were already in the family room, put her sleeping bag and hiking equipment together, and returned to the barn to check out the refrigerator and take a look at Scott's seedlings.

Cat, Nina and Eli drove to the High Health Cooperative in town to buy the food they would need. Eli swept into the market and began pointing out necessary ingredients while Cat and Nina each pushed a cart as they checked their lists. The grocery clerk said, "Having all your family for Thanksgiving?" Eli laughed and said "Yes, all my family, definitely."

With Eli making pies, Nina and Cat could make cookies from the recipe on the chocolate chip bags. Eli pointed out that they needed to make more than one kind of cookie. They decided to make sugar cookies, too. Eli shook his head.

"Good thing I'm here. I'll throw together some rum balls and confection delights like my grandmother taught me. I don't know how you two were ever wives."

Cat and Nina laughed; they were glad to have Eli's guidance in culinary matters. They also had to buy enough tea and coffee to fill the stainless steel urns they would use. There were plenty of serving platters for the turkey, stuffing, potatoes, vegetables and rolls, but they didn't have enough pie plates. Cat bought a fresh pumpkin to make the pumpkin soup she wanted to try. They would have to stop at the kitchen shop on their way home.

Thanksgiving would be the last time they would all be together. The realization quieted everyone down a bit as talk of what they would do next filtered throughout the day.

"Hey," offered Davy, "maybe after I graduate we can all get together and make a film."

"About what?" asked Eli.

"About these times, this experience, our changes that helped make change and break free of uptight old patterns...."

"And all the illegal drugs?" questioned Nina.

"Oh, Nina, what illegal drugs? Most everything we use you can grow! They're organics! If it grows in nature, how can it be illegal?" said Lenora.

"Unfortunately," said Cat, "our awareness has changed but the laws have not."

"And we are not yet the majority," added Nina.

Here they were working together one last time to make a communal meal. Lenora rolled joints in the kitchen while Nina, Cat and Eli began measuring flour in bowls and cracking eggs. They stood in a row along the kitchen counter, recipes laid out and measuring spoons and cups lined up.

From time to time, Lenora would walk over to each of them and hold a lit joint so they didn't have to stop what they were doing.

Nina sucked in a toke, "Who has the milk?" she said as she held her breath.

"Here," said Eli.

"Where's the nutmeg?" asked Cat.

"Where it always is," said Eli, "hanging in the cupboard in the little metal thingie."

"Ohhh, right," remembered Cat. When Lenora came around again, she refused any more tokes. "I need to get this done, I'm stoned enough."

They pressed on into the night, turning out six pies and dozens of cookies. Eli made two pumpkin pies, two minced meat pies, and two apple pies, and put them in the refrigerator in the barn. Catherine cleaned out the pumpkin of its meat, and placed it in a separate bowl in the barn refrigerator. She also had to refrigerate the empty pumpkin shell to keep it fresh. She couldn't wait to finish it on Thanksgiving so she could serve it at the table. She would have to time it just right, when the turkey was done and resting. It would be a perfect way to begin the meal.

Monday evening, Eddie and Amy showed up unexpectedly. Eli went to the market to get some food to cook for everyone.

On Tuesday, Davy and his housemate, Jimmy, drove to Vermont for Thanksgiving. Nina was pleased that Davy could come for a few days before she would be moving at the end of the week. It would be their last time all together at the commune. Eli went to the market to pick up the turkey he had ordered.

Good thing I got a twenty-four pounder, he thought. He was preparing oyster stuffing which no one wanted. Nina wanted a certain kind of stuffing like her mother made. Cat liked her mother's choice of Pepperidge Farm. Lenora wanted corn meal stuffing with currants cooked in a separate pan since she wouldn't be having any turkey.

Eli decided to make several kinds of stuffing in an attempt to please everyone, and knew he could make them in advance of the day. "We're having Thanksgiving dinner as close to 2:00 p.m. as possible," he announced. "I'll be getting up in the middle of the night to put the turkey in the oven, so you had all better save yourselves for it and you had all better love it!"

"We promise!" said Cat. She was going to get up early and help, too. That way they could enjoy their day when everyone came.

The day before Thanksgiving, everyone was in the kitchen getting in Eli's way. He shooed them all into the front parlor room to have the kitchen to himself. He also needed to set up the serving dishes in the dining room so it would be easier the next day.

"But its dinnertime, Eli, where will we eat?" asked Cat.

"We can eat in the kitchen at the small table," said Eli. "That way, we can serve right from the counters and clean up will be easier."

"Okay, Eli, sounds like a plan." Lenora, Nina, Davy, Jimmy and Cat crowded around the small kitchen table. Eddie and Amy sat on the floor.

Nina and Cat took out their long dresses to iron. Cat had her homemade calico dress to wear, and Nina had one she made from Merimekko fabric. Cat offered to iron one of Paul's togas while Paul was filling the pie shells to be baked. Eddie vacuumed the parlor, dining room and entryway. Eli wouldn't allow him into the kitchen.

Amy was assigned 'paraphernalia pick up' throughout the downstairs with orders to find all the pipes stuck in coffee mugs, and rolling papers in the kitchen drawers, as well as in the knick knacks on the window sills. Eli wanted pipes and papers ready for dessert and gathered together in the family room. He envisioned everyone being full and ready to sit around before the fire while he presented his beautiful pies and goodies. He couldn't have been more wrong if he had ordered a UFO to land on the roof.

At 5:00 a.m. on Thanksgiving morning, Eli placed the turkey in the oven, yawned and returned to bed. At 5:45 a.m., Cat woke up and stumbled down the staircase to the kitchen to find the turkey already in the oven. She went back to bed.

At 9:00 a.m., the doorbell rang. Cat couldn't imagine who it was since no one used the doorbell. She came down the stairs in her flannel nightgown and looked out the side windows. It was a man in uniform she didn't recognize and Deputy Shepherd. Cat couldn't understand what they would be doing there Thanksgiving morning. She opened the door.

"Good morning, Mrs. Janson," began Deputy Shepherd. "This is Chief Bronson."

"How do you do?" said Cat.

"M'am," continued Deputy Shepherd, "we're sorry to tell you that we'd like to search your premises for illegal drugs."

Cat felt the color drain out of her face. "Whhaa—aat?"

"Please step aside," said Chief Bronson.

Cat slammed the door and locked it, sliding a bolt into place.

"I take that as a 'no'," said Deputy Shepherd.

Chief Bronson sighed, and then yelled through the door. "Mrs. Janson, we'll get a search warrant and be back! I was trying not to ruin the whole day!"

As soon as they left, Cat ran through the house to secure all the doors, including through the family room, and into the barn to check that the plank was slid across the barn doors. She thought about how much time Scott was at the commune, and went upstairs in the barn to the second floor. Great, green bushes were hanging upside down along one wall. She went up to the third floor. There were some green bales that looked like the hay they had for last summer's garden. Cat paused, walked over to them, and didn't have to smell too much of their odor to recognize it wasn't.

She ran down the two flights of stairs, through the family room and into the house, calling, "Everybody up! Everybody up! We have an emergency!" She telephoned Jessica and Gene, and when Gene answered, yelled, "Where's Scott?!?"

"Right here," Gene said.

"Put him on!"

"Sure, all right. Scott?" Gene said, sounds of the phone being passed.

"Hello?" said Scott.

"Hello my ass!" yelled Cat. "You have 10 minutes to get over here and get every shred of your 'plant farm' out of my barn and out of my life! The police were just here and are coming back with a search warrant!"

"Whaa-at? Oh, shit!"

"Hurry up! Now!" yelled Cat.

By this time, everyone was coming down the front stairs and the back stairs, fuzzyheaded and bleary-eyed.

Nina's eyes were wide open having heard the conversation. She reached toward Cat. They hugged.

"All right, let's take care of this everyone!" Nina said. "Eli, get the vacuum cleaner and a couple of extra bags. Eddie and Amy, you take the family room and loft. Davy and I will do the upstairs in the house. Lenora, you start in the downstairs and meet up with Eli. Let's go!"

Eli went to the closet and grabbed the vacuum cleaner with the brush attachment. Eddie and Amy went immediately into the family room and climbed the ladder into the loft. They had been stashing hash there for months behind an old beam. Fortunately, as part of the plan for the next day and the fact that everyone was moving out, the marijuana plus all the little pipes and extra rolling papers that tended to be placed on the mantel, up on top of window sills, and in cupboards, had been gathered together in a large, wooden bowl. But, Eddie and Amy took no chances now. They went through everything in the family room just to be sure.

Nina and Davy went upstairs and pulled out a shoebox under the bed where they usually kept an ounce of pot. They opened bureau drawers and took out package after package of rolling papers; they seemed to be everywhere. They checked the kids' bedrooms, on top of an armoire in the hall, any place someone might have stashed something away for a rainy day. Then, they went along the back hallway, as there were nooks and crannies that would hold small boxes or containers. When everyone had run out of marijuana, they would always come to Nina. It seemed she always had a little container someplace. No one went into the attic as it was filled with old relics from earlier days, mismatched bed parts, a few old headboards, some metal lantern parts, so no worries there. Or were there? Just in case, they pushed open the overhead door and climbed through.

Eli took the vacuum cleaner up the back stairs in time to see Nina and Davy disappear into the attic. "What are you guys doing?"

"Being extra-cautious," Nina called back.

"I'm beginning vacuuming, now," said Eli, "I will be vacuuming everything, and I do mean everything."

"Fine," Nina called.

Eli plugged the vacuum in and began in the girls' bedroom starting with windowsills, under the bed, tops of furniture, and finally the old floorboards. He worked his way through the entire upstairs cleaning baseboards, inside beds, checking under mattresses and inside every closet.

Cat had grabbed a box of black garbage bags and headed for the barn. She unceremoniously swept the trays of seedlings into the bags, and then began pulling down the hanging bushes. The recent snow fall piled against the outside barn doors was holding them shut, and there was no time to shovel it away. *How am I going to get this shit out of here?* Cat wondered. Once Eddie and Amy were finished with the family room, they came to the barn to help. Then Lenora, having finished the rooms downstairs, joined them.

"Okay, you guys put these 'hay bales' into garbage bags, then tie them up. Help me open up the window here—we're going to have to push all these bags out the window. There's no other way."

"What if someone comes?"

"It better be Scott," Cat said. "I just hope that no one drives up the road."

Just then, the sound of a whining engine coming up the hill drew their attention. They were leaning out the third floor window of the barn and saw Gene's truck crest the hill.

"Thank God," said Cat. "I have a good mind to load up my shotgun."

With that, they began pushing the bags out the window, one after the other, as Gene and Scott backed up the truck, trying to get closer to the barn in the snowdrifts. The truck slid and rocked in the snow, but they were able to back it up somewhat, and Scott immediately jumped out and began yelling at Cat.

"What are you doing? You're going to ruin my crop!"

"You're lucky I don't shoot you!" yelled Cat. "Nina and I could both lose our children because of your stupidity! Get your bags of shit out of here before the police come back!"

Gene and Scott grabbed the bags as they fell to the snow and loaded them in the back of the truck bed. There were more than a dozen when all was finished and Eli began vacuuming the barn starting on the third floor. It was cold, but everyone was sweating from the adrenalined effort they were making to clear the place of seeds and all the evidence of what had been growing there.

Nina and Davy had closed up the attic, satisfied that nothing had ever made it up there, and did a thorough room search once more. They began with all the bedrooms in the house, then the downstairs and all the closets and cubbies, then the family room and storage areas, and finally to the barn.

At one point, Nina said to Davy, "I don't know what I'll do if I lose my boys."

"I have an idea," said Davy, "what if we aren't here when the police come back."

"That would be good for me, but what about Cat?"

"It's her home," said Davy, "she will be blamed anyway."

Nina felt torn. If she wasn't there and they found something, then she couldn't be arrested. *But,* she thought, *if I am...*

The farm looked like a beehive, people running around in pajamas with sweaters over them and their Sorel boots. Up into the barn, down into the family room, through the kitchen, even the front porch rafters were checked. Finally the truck was loaded and Gene and Scott drove away. Sam passed them heading to the farm for Thanksgiving dinner.

"What's going on?" Sam asked as he entered the family room door.

A quick explanation followed and he asked what he could do.

Eli was in the family room now, an extension cord hanging over the loft so he could vacuum all the floorboards and cross beams there. Sam helped him with the brush attachments and plugged in the extension cord while Amy rolled up the rug in front of the fireplace to check for seeds. Nina and Davy gathered all the pipes, papers, baggies and anything else they could think of that looked like drug paraphernalia and put it in the trunk of Nina's Datsun. Jimmy did another look into high places and moved some of the furniture so they could look under it.

"Nina, you and Davy drive the Datsun over to Gene and Jessica's and stay there," Cat said.

"No, Cat, I'd rather be here with you," Nina said.

"Not an option. If they can search the premises that means your car, too. If you're not here, you'll have less chance of anything happening. There's nothing I can do about it, it's my home."

Davy came over to Nina and said, "Let's just go, and empty the trunk! I don't want to get stopped!"

"I'll do that," Nina said," but I'm coming back, Cat."

"Actually, I really think everyone should leave. That way, I'll be the only one who gets busted."

Everyone gathered around Cat. Eli had finished the family room and was standing with a vacuum cleaner hose in one hand. "Listen up! Back up the cars and we'll plug in the extension cord and run it out the door—we can do this people!"

Statements of, "We're staying, Cat," and "We're not going anywhere and leave you to face this alone," and "We're here," were murmured as they all came and hugged Cat. Sam was last, and held her close, "We'll get through this," he said, looking into her eyes.

Cat wiped away tears and turned to Eli, "Have you checked the turkey?"

"Omigod!" Eli said as he ran into the kitchen and yanked open the oven door. Lenora ran after him and fished the glass turkey baster out of a drawer.

"Here, Eli, do your perverted thing," Lenora said.

The telephone rang and Cat answered it.

"Hello?"

"Happy Thanksgiving, Mommy," said Laura.

"Happy Thanksgiving, honey, how are you, sweetheart?" Cat replied.

"Good, we're having a great big turkey, and we made little boots for the legs!" said Laura.

"Nice, honey, sounds like fun," Cat's silent tears ran down her face as she tried to keep her voice light.

"Here's Becky," Laura said handing her little sister the phone.

"Mommy?" Becky said.

"Yes, sweetie," Cat said, weeping now.

"Mommy, we made a jello mold with Grammy!" said Becky.

"Great, honey, that's great!"

"Okay, bye-bye, Mommy!"

"Bye, Becky." Cat listened after the phone clicked off. She wondered what Daniel was thinking, if he had put his attorney up to this raid, or if it was his attorney's idea of catching her with illegal drugs while Daniel had the girls. If he had put the children up to calling her to see if she was there, or had been arrested, was something she would never know. If she didn't get arrested, she would get the girls back directly after Thanksgiving weekend. No way would she let them stay with him now.

"We're going to make this a great Thanksgiving," said Eli. He went to the barn to check the pies in the refrigerator. In the freezer compartment, he found another ounce of pot. He stuffed it in his pocket. Then, Lenora remembered that in the herbs and spices jars, several were filled with pot because it looked like oregano. When Eli came back to the kitchen, he looked defeated. Lenora and he exchanged worried glances.

"The damn stuff is everywhere," he said in a low voice.

"I know," said Lenora, "I just remembered the herb jars."

"All right, listen up," said Eli. Everyone gathered in the kitchen expecting assignments for cooking and preparation.

"We have a problem. Think about if there are any other areas where you could have stashed some pot aside."

Cat looked like she was going to faint. From under the kitchen sink, Eli grabbed a paper bag, "Here, Cat," he said, "sit down and breathe into this."

Cat sat in a kitchen chair, tried to breathe, and then put her head between her legs. Nina rubbed her neck. "Cat, Davy and I had better take the car to Jessica and Gene's now. We'll be back as soon as we unload the trunk. The rest of it is clean."

Cat couldn't speak.

"It's over," she said dejectedly.

"No, it's not," said Sam. He kneeled down in front of Cat and took her hands.

Eddie stood at the kitchen counter, looking up at the snow-covered meadow behind the house. "I have an idea," he said.

"What?" asked Amy.

"I can bury anything else we find in the snow at the end of the road. It's off the property. No one can prove it was here. I've had enough skirmishes to know how they play this game."

For a moment, everyone forgot that Eddie and Amy were drug dealers. Then Cat said, "Is this why this happened? Are they following you?"

"I—I don't think so," Eddie said, slowly shaking his head, eyes lowered.

Davy said, "We should go and unload the trunk at Gene's. Put everything else you have in the trunk and we'll take it away."

Eli pulled the baggie out of his pocket. Lenora handed over the jars from the herb drawer. Not wanting to take any chances, she pulled open the drawer and handed it to Davy. He and Nina went outside and put these new findings in the trunk. For good measure, Eli threw the vacuum cleaner in, too.

"Oh, the medicine chest!" Davy said and dashed back into the house, ran upstairs to the bathroom and opened the medicine cabinet. On the top shelf behind the Vicks Vaporub, there was a tiny pillbox. He opened it and took two of the pills inside and swallowed them, and pocketed the box. Then, he ran downstairs, "I remembered my Quaaludes, thank God," and with that ran out to the car.

When Nina poked her head in the doorway of the family room to say 'be right back,' before joining Davy, the phone rang. It was Cat's lawyer, William Farley.

"What the hell is going on down there?" he boomed.

"The police came to search the house and said they would return with a search warrant." Cat replied.

"And, you didn't call me. I had to learn it from the county judge where Mutt and Jeff went to get the warrant?"

"I needed to make sure the farm was clean of anything suspicious," Cat chose her words carefully.

"Well, you're off the hook this time. Fortunately, I know the judge a lot better that those two dingbats in your town."

"What?" asked Cat, coming up out of the deep pit she was in.

"Happy Thanksgiving, and call me Monday. Your husband is starting to piss me off." Click.

Cat was frozen still with the phone poised next to her ear.

...There walks a lady we all know
Who shines white light and wants to show
How everything still turns to gold...
And shes buying a stairway to heaven...

Robert Plant and Jimmy Page, Led Zeppelin,
"Stairway to Heaven," *Led Zeppelin IV*, 1971

Chapter 16

"Group hug," said Eli after Cat explained the phone call. "Now, let's get this Thanksgiving dinner underway!"

Nina felt relieved as well, and asked Cat: "What about calling Gene and Jessica and inviting them for dinner? Maybe this whole thing wasn't Scott's fault after all—maybe the police got pushed by Daniel's attorneys."

"You can call them," Cat said. "I'm still too angry at Scott, but Gene and Jessica can come for dinner."

"And leave Scott home alone?"

"Yes," said Cat, "he can smoke himself into oblivion for all I care." Cat was thinking that she couldn't empty the farm of everyone soon enough. Eddie and Amy were leaving tomorrow, and she hadn't even considered what part they might have played in a drug bust scenario. *They're probably wanted all over the United States*, Cat thought.

She would have to check the wanted posters in the post office Monday. And it wasn't just that Scott had set up his own little business in the barn; *she* hadn't checked on it. She was as mad at herself as she was everyone else who might have contributed to what could have happened. Her blind trust had really hurt her.

Lenora set the table in the dining room while Eli cooked, and stirred, and clucked over the stove as he checked on and basted the turkey. He made gravy from the pan scrapings and asked Cat about the pumpkin soup.

"Screw the pumpkin soup," Cat said.

Eddie and Amy sat in the family room and discussed their own future. "This could have been it for us," Eddie said to Amy. "I know," she replied. "Or, we could be the reason this all happened to Cat."

They decided to pull up stakes and leave today. It was time to hit the road and change their lives. California, maybe. Or perhaps, they should go to Canada.

Just as they were thinking of leaving, Gene and Jessica with Scott in tow entered the family room.

Eddie looked up. "I don't think Scott's welcome here," he said.

"I know, I know" said Gene, "but he owes Cat an apology and then we'll leave if she wants us to."

Eddie and Amy followed them into the kitchen. Cat sat at the table with a steaming mug of chamomile tea Eli had made for her. Sam sat next to her, one hand rubbing her shoulders. When she looked up at Scott, a steely glint flashed in her eyes.

"Cat, I'm sorry," said Scott, even looking sorry, his hair lank and swinging forward around his face.

"You, you—" Cat began.

"Really, really, I mean it, I am so-o-o-o sorry, please forgive me." Scott said.

Cat said, "All right, Scott, all right, but I won't get over being angry at you any time soon."

"I don't blame you, Cat," Scott replied.

Sam took her hand. "How're you doing?" he asked.

Cat looked at Sam and shrugged. "I guess I'm okay."

A thump-thump-thump sound came down the front stairs. "What's that?" Cat asked.

Sam stood up and walked to the front room and into the hallway. Sitting on the bottom step was Davy looking totally goofy.

"What's going on Dave?" asked Sam.

"The Quaaludes kicked in," Davy said.

"You should have saved one for Cat."

The turkey was done, Eli carved, everyone assembled at the long, dining table to share a last dinner together. It was bittersweet with all the events of the morning. No one dared to go out to the car for a joint, but at least they had plenty of wine that Eli had chosen for the occasion. The only fully stoned person was Davy who kept falling off his chair. Jimmy lit the candles on the table and Lenora carried out dish after dish.

Eli stood at the head of the table, "I propose a toast, here's to endings and beginnings, and may we all meet again—"

Someone was pounding on the front door. Cat's heart jumped into her throat and when she stood up, her chair fell over.

Sam stood up with her, "I'll get it, Cat," he said.

"No, no, I'll go."

Sam followed Cat to the door.

She looked through the side panes of glass. It was two men who looked remarkably like the bongo-playing Kentucky brothers. She opened the door. It *was* the bongo-playing Kentucky brothers. Cat began to laugh.

Bobby Ray brightened when the door opened and began, "We heard the commune was sold. Will it be a real commune now?"

Cat laughed until she cried. "No, no, it will probably never be a commune," she said, wiping her eyes.

Bobby Ray turned to his brother, Bobby Joe, "Well, Bobby Joe, what do you have to say for yourself?"

Sam laughed and they held the door open together, inviting Bobby Ray and Bobby Joe in for Thanksgiving dinner.

As they all stuffed themselves and drank the wonderful wine for each course Eli had prepared, Cat felt a beginning sense of calm as well as being very grateful that she had survived this day without going to jail. She knew that once she had her daughters back home, she would feel much better. *But, where was she going to live?*

It was still early but overcast and it wouldn't be light much longer. Eddie and Amy spoke to everyone at the table, and said it was time that they left. There wouldn't be anyway anyone could get in touch with them as they had decided to make some changes in their lives. Heads turned questioningly toward them.

"We're going straight," Eddie said, almost sounding a little proud.

"Gollllleeee, gee," said Bobby Ray. "Are you on the lamb or somethin'?"

"Never mind," said Cat. "The less said the better?" She looked at Eddie and then Amy.

"Yup. Amy and I need to make some changes in our lives and we may be leaving the country."

Eli raised his glass, "Here, here!"

Congratulations followed. Eddie and Amy stood up, went around the table to say their goodbyes to everyone, and then Cat and Sam walked them to the door.

After they left, Sam turned Cat around to face him, and kissed her long and hard.

Cat didn't know what to say, so she didn't say anything but walked back into the dining room.

More pie was passed around, and Gene, Jessica and Scott said it was time to go. They said to Nina and Davy, "See you guys tomorrow?"

"Sure, we'll be over sometime tomorrow as I have to drive Davy, Jimmy, Lenora and Eli to Cambridge and pick up the kids Saturday," said Nina.

"Sounds good. Thanks, Cat, Eli, everyone for such great food," said Gene.

"We'll see you around, Cat," Jessica said, "you'll be here another month, right?"

"Yes, but let me walk you to the barn, there's a few things of yours you can take home with you."

They went into the barn and Gene and Jessica gathered up their belongings left from months before, then hugged everyone good-bye and went out the family room door. Scott said he was sorry again. Cat nodded.

It was time to clear the table and put the food away. Eli supervised the process; then he and Lenora sat in the family room after building a nice fire.

"Quite a day," Eli said to Lenora.

"I'm exhausted," Lenora said, "I'm going to bed."

Bobby Joe and Bobby Ray ambled into the family room and sat on either side of the wide fireplace, staring into the flames. "Well, at least this time we have enough money to get back to Kentucky," said Bobby Ray.

"Maybe we should go someplace else," said Bobby Joe. "I heard there's a commune startin' in Maine."

"You hear a lot of things," said Bobby Ray. "I'm thinkin' your hearin' ain't too good."

Nina and Davy sat in the front parlor on the sofa holding each other, their energy drained after the day's events—and Davy's taking Quaaludes. They noticed the lights going on in the barn windows.

Cat had brought Sam up to the second floor where his tepee was stored. As she pointed out how it had to be removed by the weekend, Sam reached for her and spun her around. They were perfectly framed in the window facing the front room with suffused golden light glowing behind them. Nina and Davy watched while Sam and Cat began to kiss. After awhile, they slipped from view. Nina and Davy looked at each other. "Uh-oh," Davy said.

The next morning arrived sunny and clear, and breathtakingly cold. Eli put up sandwiches for the Kentucky brothers, whom he referred to as the "Kentucky Wonders," and sent them on their way. Then Nina and Davy brought their things, mostly the rest of Nina's belongings, to Gene and Jessica's log cabin. They returned for Jimmy, Lenora and Eli.

"Once I get settled again, you'll have to come and visit," said Cat to Eli and Lenora. "Oh, I will," said Eli, but did you know Lenora is joining the Peace Corps?"

"Lenora!" everyone said at once.

Nina said, "You never mentioned it!"

"Things got a little busy this week, in case you don't remember," Lenora laughed. "Besides, it's time I stopped talking about how things need to change and started doing something about it."

Nina took Cat aside, "What are you doing with Sam?"

"I'm not sure," Cat said.

"I'll call you when I get back on Sunday," said Nina.

"That'd be good, Nina, please do," said Cat.

Everyone hugged Cat and Sam, not wanting to leave him out of the equation. Then, they were gone. Cat and Sam stood in the doorway like parents watching grown children leaving for college—which it seemed that some of them were.

"Well, it's done." Cat said.

"Let's have a cup of coffee," Sam said. "We need to talk."

...But only love can break your heart
Try to be sure right from the start
Yes only love can break your heart
What if your world should fall apart? . . .

Neil Young, back up by Crazy Horse,
"Only Love Can Break Your Heart,"
After the Goldrush, 1970

Chapter 17

Cat felt all at sea. She and Sam had made love on the cold floor of the barn last night in winter wool coats and Sorel boots. *What, on earth, is there to talk about?* She didn't think Cheryl could get any more aggravated with her than she already must be. Unless they had some open relationship that they were able to truly embrace.

"Cat, Cheryl is away on purpose. She knows I wanted to be with you."

"Yeah, well you've *been* with me," Cat replied.

"I mean more than that. We both think with all that you're going through over the custody battle and the farm being sold that you should come live with us in our big winter house. In the spring or early summer, we'll be setting up a tepee and I could help you get your own tepee together. We could live on the land that I have that's been in my family for hundreds of years. I just have to put a better road in once the snow melts and it dries out. A brook runs the full length of one side of the property, deep enough to swim in, and there are springs for drinking water, and we could have an organic garden together. Maybe we could start a real community. What do you say?"

Cat was so surprised; you could have pushed her over with a feather. "I don't know what to say yet, I will have to think about it, Sam."

"Well, let's try this. Move into our winter home. There's plenty of room for the girls, and I could drive them to their school in town every morning on my way to work. Then, they wouldn't have to change schools."

"And, Cheryl thinks this is a good idea?"

"It was her idea to begin with," said Sam.

"Including us having sex?" asked Cat.

"Not exactly, but—" Sam started.

"Sam! You talk to Cheryl again after she returns. Then, we'll see."

Cat realized she had fallen hard for Sam. All the teasing she had taken from Eli seemed to be true. He warned her she would love someone she couldn't have.

Over the weekend, Sam and Cheryl talked. When Sam returned to the commune on Saturday to tell Cat, she was on her way back from Boston after picking up Laura and Becky. They stopped on their way home for dinner as Cat hadn't left the commune since Thanksgiving and needed to shop for fresh food. She had Monday off and planned to go to the High Health Food Cooperative after taking the girls to school.

Nina called her, but she was in transit. Sam was sitting in his truck, parked in the side yard when Cat pulled in Saturday evening.

Cat was surprised to see him and tooted her horn as she pulled in.

"Hi, Sam, what are you doing here?" asked Cat, as she got out of the Jeep and helped the girls get out on the other side.

"I wanted to catch up on a few things," Sam said. "Hi, Laura, hi, Becky, how was your vacation?"

"Okay" said Laura. "Mom, you said when we got home you would play Parcheesi with us."

"And, I will," said Cat. "Sam, my girls have been gone all week. I really want to spend time with them tonight."

"I understand," said Sam. "I know how to play Parcheesi."

Becky smiled at Sam. "That will be fun!" she said.

Becky was fine with Sam being there. Laura just said, "All right."

Cat unlocked the front door, put on all the lights, and got the Parcheesi game out of the family room, which would be too cold to play in. She set it up on the dining room table. Sam carried in the girls' bags from the back of the Jeep, and went into the dining room to help set up the game while Cat started heating water for tea.

She put out little bowls of crackers and Laughing Cow cheese. The girls loved the little cubes because they were just the right size for their fingers.

They sat at the table and played Parcheesi. Laura won and she was happy with the way it turned out after all.

Cat took the girls upstairs to get them ready for bed, ran a warm bath, and rubbed them down with big towels so she could hug them both. "I missed you so much, Laura," she said.

Laura smiled.

Then, "I missed you so much, Becky," Cat said.

"I missed you, too, Momma," Becky said.

After she read to the girls and settled them in their bed, she returned to the dining room where Sam was sitting, drinking a cup of tea.

"What's going on, Sam?" Cat asked.

"Cheryl wants you and the girls to move in with us. She's fine about...about everything." Sam said.

"That might be all right, but do you really think it would work?"

"Tomorrow we'd like you all to come over and spend the day with us. We'll be doing some chores, chopping wood, but that's all. It'll give the girls a chance to check out the house," said Sam.

"That might be fun for the girls," Cat said, smiling. "I look forward to coming over Sunday, and we'll see how it goes."

"Great," Sam said, and stood up. "I think it would be a good thing." He carried his tea mug out to the kitchen sink, touching Cat on the shoulder as he walked by.

She walked to the kitchen and followed Sam to the front door. He turned and gave her a hug good night. Then, as Cat hugged him back, he kissed her hard on the mouth. She kissed him hard on the mouth, and they were back in the front room, holding each other close and fondling each other through their clothes.

"Oh, Sam, how could we live with you if this is what's going to happen all the time?" Cat asked.

Sam smiled. "We'll think of something."

Cat closed the hall door by the stairs, closed the door to the kitchen and shut off the light in the front room. A couple of hours later, Sam left.

Sunday dawned bright and wintry, more snow had fallen the night before and Cat pushed it off the front porch with a broom. When Laura and Becky got up, Cat was already dressed and humming to herself in the kitchen.

"Good morning, Momma!" said Laura.

"Good morning, starshine! Ready for breakfast?"

"I am," said Laura

"Me, too," said Becky.

Cat whipped up some pancakes and chopped apple to mix into the batter. It was the girls' favorite breakfast. Then, she cooked an egg for each one and placed it on top of the stack. She heated maple syrup that they had gotten from Jed's farm on the wood stove and served it in a pottery pitcher. She would have to stop by and tell him they were leaving. Between finding her on the road that fateful day and recommending Attorney Farley, she had a lot to thank him for.

"Today we're going to Sam and Cheryl's house to visit," Cat said.

"When are we going to get a television like Daddy's?" asked Laura.

"Not any time soon," answered Cat.

The day went well visiting Sam and Cheryl. The girls liked all the pets that they had, a big Golden Retriever dog, a female cat that had recently given birth to three adorable kittens, and a parrot they were babysitting for the house owners that talked and squawked enough to make Cheryl put a cover over the cage to quiet him down.

The dog doted on the girls, and followed them around the house. When he lay down, he let the kittens crawl all over him. Laura and Becky were delighted. Cheryl let them hold the kittens, they had never held kittens before, and they each wanted one for their very own.

"I like the orange one," said Becky.

"I like the one with all different colors," said Laura.

"That's called a calico cat," said Cheryl.

The girls put their faces into the kittens' fur and carried them around the house.

Late in the afternoon, Cat and the girls went back to the commune. It was so quiet now with everyone gone, it felt empty for just the three of them.

They had supper, and as Cat was putting them to bed, the girls asked when they could go back to Cheryl and Sam's.

She went down the back stairs, thinking she would get a book to read in the family room.

The phone in the hallway began to ring by the time she set foot on the bottom stair.

"Hello?"

"Catherine?"

"Yes?"

"Attorney Farley here. We have a date for the depositions in my offices."

"So, this is it, then. When?"

"Tomorrow."

"What?!?"

"Don't tell yourself bad stories about this, now. It's going to be fine. You should know, however, that your doctor, Dr. Bernstein, has offered to testify against you, but I am pleased with all the information we have gathered from Dr. Lindberg. Now, get a good night's rest and I'll see you at 8:00 a.m."

"Is that the time they start—8:00 a.m.?"

"Nope. Depositions start at 10:00 a.m. but I know better than not to be ready. Be here early and, Catherine, stop worrying!"

"I'll try."

She immediately called Nina at Jessica and Gene's to ask if she could bring the girls over before school because the day of the depositions had arrived. After expressing all of her concerns about the depositions, Nina told her to "be strong." *Whatever that means*, thought Cat.

Catherine went to bed in a state of heightened anxiety. She kept trying to sleep, but all she could see was the empty house, the empty rooms, and then her feelings of dread from the past when Daniel had taken her daughters.

...Round and round and round we spin,
To weave a wall to hem us in,
It won't be long, it won't be long...

> Neil Young,
>> "Round & Round (It Won't Be Long)"
>>> *Everybody Knows This Is Nowhere,* 1969

Chapter 18

Cat didn't like having to drive to Montpelier so early. All her thoughts kept returning to Dr. Bernstein taking her husband's side. Even before they had moved to Vermont that summer, he had suggested that she go into a mental hospital for "observation." Catherine didn't trust him after that. Between his prescriptions that made her feel worse and his siding with Daniel, Catherine had felt totally alone. It had been a relief when she left for Vermont to know she wouldn't have to see him again. *My own doctor offering to testify against me! What a prick!*

In spite of her mother-in-law's opinion that she needed to be in counseling, Catherine felt that her doctor was wrong about her. Looking back, Catherine knew she was ahead of her time, but she also knew acquiescing to what she thought of as the dominant male scenario was wrong. She had rights as a human being. Her need to steer her life in her own best interests was being put aside by men who wanted her to defer to them. She was going against the grain of long-standing tradition in both her own family and her husband's.

Knowing that Daniel would play the crazy card to get custody of the girls didn't help her confidence. She only hoped there wasn't enough evidence to prove it. Her own emotional outbreaks, her own conflicts of motherhood and working, her own unsettled desires to have a summer home and then choose to stay there all year—all of this could add up to her being seen as unstable. Not to mention that it became a commune.

She had brought all of this on herself. *Once you take a stand for something,* she thought, *you will have to either see it through or accept the consequences.* And, *I am not giving up.* In her intense need for the freedom to live her own life, Catherine wasn't sure if she was playing Russian roulette with custody. *What if Daniel proves me unfit and has me institutionalized? What if they fill me full of drugs like I have read about in the newspapers?* The law that allowed institutionalization for observation was being challenged because some people were kept in institutions for months only later to be proven mentally stable.[18] But, the law hadn't been changed. All it would take was a respected opinion to the court and they could put her away. A recent movie that had been based on a story about a husband sending his wife to a mental institution time and again for shock treatments had frightened Catherine.

The time for the depositions had finally come, but Catherine wished she didn't have to go. She knew it wouldn't look right if she wasn't there. Attorney Farley had prepared his questions for Daniel by detailing every past item of anything that sounded like abuse—from not allowing her to do things on her own or make her own decisions, to going against her thoughts or ideas when she spoke in front of other people. Her psychiatrist, Dr. Lindberg, was also to be present, and the plan was for two days of depositions—filling Catherine with dread. She got lost twice while driving even though she had certainly been there enough to remember how to get there. Her attorney wanted her to arrive early enough to avoid running into her husband and his entourage. And entourage it was.

Catherine checked in at the desk, it was just 8:30 a.m., and as she looked out the window to the parking lot, she could see a long, black limousine pull up in front of the building. Her stomach sank.

Daniel was sitting in the back seat of the limousine as they drove to Montpelier from Boston. He couldn't believe how unsettled he felt. Somehow, it had all blown out of proportion, and he was getting divorced from the woman he loved. He would have to be grilled during the depositions although his attorney's made light of it. One of the attorneys said, "Some 'hayseed' whose tactics work in the country isn't going to unseat Daniel Janson. Nosirree! Daniel, you will be just fine."

Daniel didn't feel fine. In fact, he didn't know what he was doing anymore. He had hired the best attorneys he knew for his particular divorce, and he had his wife's doctor on his side. There didn't seem to be much more that needed to be done. The threat of Catherine losing the children would bring her to her knees, he was sure of it. And, now that he had a cooler head about it all, he wasn't sure that he wanted to do that to her. *Even if I can prove her unfit, do I want to have her institutionalized? Do I really want to try and put her away?*

As they pulled into the parking lot, one of his attorney's guffawed, "Nice place."

"I hope there aren't any chickens in the offices!" another one chimed in.

"Oh, this ought to be good," said a third.

The two accompanying clerks grinned. They were the carriers of the documents for the three attorneys Daniel had hired. All of them would cost Daniel a pretty penny for these two days. Not to mention staying at a hotel and dining out. At least the limousine was from his law practice, and he could write it off as a business expense. The driver had been prepped to wait for them all day and assumed that they would be going to lunch around noon.

It was 8:30 a.m. when they pulled into the parking lot, although the depositions did not begin until 10:00 a.m. His attorney's wanted to be early to put Catherine's attorney off guard.

"Just as I figured," Attorney William Farley said to Catherine as he watched the limo pull up. "More than an hour early. That's fine. I have the court reporter setting up in the conference room already, and my paralegal, Jenny, is there as well."

He called to one of the legal secretaries, "Would you put out the tray of bagels and pitchers of water? The coffee urn is already in there, just needs to be plugged in." He turned to Catherine, "I put it in there this morning planning on this." He continued, "Let's wait in my office until 10 o'clock. Let them stew a bit."

He poked his head in the conference room to call to the psychiatrist. "Come on, Dr. Lindberg, the other lawyers are here, so we'll leave them to the conference room. Jenny, would you close the door after they enter? Then join us in my office. We'll meet there until it's time."

Dr. Lindberg, Catherine and Attorney Farley headed down the hall away from the conference room to the opposite side of the building.

It had taken months to get the depositions held at Catherine's attorney's offices. Daniel's attorneys wanted them held in Boston, but William Farley wouldn't budge. Several times meetings were scheduled and subsequently rescheduled because he would not let Catherine go to Boston. Attorney Farley had been very specific about her not leaving the state of Vermont for any reason, and Catherine knew it had everything to do with her being served in Massachusetts which could have thrown the divorce back into Daniel's ballpark.

It was finally 10:00 a.m. and time to begin. In the conference room, Daniel was watching the clock. He would be deposed first. All the times he had questioned witnesses to exact what he wanted from them was haunting him as he awaited his moment. But, Daniel didn't really think Catherine's one-horse attorney could have as good a strategy as his team. He noticed a young woman placing boxes at the other end of the table, and couldn't help feeling a tiny bit smug.

Catherine's legs trembled as she walked down the hall flanked by Dr. Lindberg and Attorney Farley as his paralegal, Jenny, came out of the conference room to get another box of documents. Catherine was aware of the discrepancy in the appearance of her attorney and Daniel's attorneys. They were suited Boston-proper. No doubt their suits were Brooks

Brothers with silk Windsor-knot ties and cuff-linked shirts. They looked pressed and immaculate and out of place in the simple conference room with a rustic pine table, polished as it was.

Attorney Farley had on a wash-and-wear shirt, a tie that didn't meet his waistband, but curved over his broad stomach, and there was a thread hanging from the hem of his jacket. It made Catherine want to groan. Upon Farley's group's entrance, everyone stood and introductions were made.

Catherine glanced at Daniel as she approached the table. She had already been told she was to sit at the far end of the table on the side, to the left of Attorney Farley and to the right of Dr. Lindberg, whose presence would shield her from Daniel's clerks and attorney's. They took up half the seats at the other end of the table. The opposing side would not have a direct view of Catherine.

Jenny asked Catherine if she would like coffee and poured it for their small group while papers were rustling and the court reporter was getting ready. She sat at a separate desk alongside the window facing the meadow. Attorney Farley stood up, reached for a bagel, smothered it in cream cheese and began the depositions by asking, "Everyone all set?" He took a bite, chewed noisily, and before it was swallowed, started the formalities.

"First, I want to thank you for coming here for the depositions," he said, nodding toward Daniel and the attorneys and clerks. "I recognize that you are doing me a favor, as you pointed out, by coming to us instead of us going to you." With that he smiled, showing all of his teeth and quite a bit of cream cheese.

"State your name for the record, please."

"My name is Daniel Janson."

"Address? Home and work, please."

Daniel gave his home address as their home in Boston, and his work address in downtown Boston.

The questions droned on, Catherine barely listening, as she was lulled by the sound of voices going back and forth like an endless tennis match on a hot summer day. All she could think about was that tomorrow was her turn. *Tomorrow is my turn. Tomorrow is my turn.* Over and over, she thought about what she would be asked. *How will I ever live through this?* Catherine wondered.

Then she heard Daniel's lawyers protest. She looked at Farley pacing about and saying, "Did you tell her she could or could not return to work?"

"I told her not to do it." Daniel answered.

"And, her doctor?" Farley asked.

"He told her she shouldn't leave our newborn daughter so soon."

"And then what happened?"

"Catherine returned to work. Our British nanny took care of our girls."

"And did anything happen as a result of her returning to her job?" Did the children suffer? Did anyone go hungry?"

"No," Daniel said.

"In fact, wasn't she happier than when she had just a focus inside the home?"

"Well, yes, I guess—" Daniel began.

"Yes or no, please."

"Yes," Daniel said.

One of his attorneys then intervened, "These are depositions. Mr. Janson can speak about it more than with just a 'yes' or 'no'."

"I realize that, thank you," Attorney Farley said. Then he smothered another half of a bagel with cream cheese, paused to take a large bite out of it and turned toward Daniel to continue while chewing away, mouth open.

"She graduated at the top of her class, didn't she? And was immediately hired by one of the best interior and architectural design firms in Boston, wasn't she? At nearly the same salary you were earning at the time you started your own business, wasn't it?"

"That's three questions," objected one of Daniel's attorneys lamely.

"Go ahead, answer all three," Farley said while noisily chewing.

Hours passed. It was time to break for lunch. There would be an hour's time in between. "It'll take them two hours," Farley joked, "after they head all the way back into Montpelier to find a restaurant."

Catherine wanted to lay down someplace, but instead she had to sit on one of the stuffed chairs in Farley's office. She just wasn't sure how things were really doing. Farley, upon entering the office, closed the door after Jenny and Dr. Lindberg. Then, he went into the kitchen to retrieve their lunches.

"This will be fine," Farley said, "This is really going well, but I don't want to be overly optimistic. We'll see what they pull out this afternoon when I get down to details."

"What kind of details?" asked Catherine.

"We have to go over the perception of the farm, the time everyone moved in after Daniel moved out, what the locals said, all that."

"What *who* said?"

"Oh, you know, the townspeople. I had Jenny spend some time talking to the people to get their opinions."

"You did? Why didn't you tell me?"

"I didn't want to be blindsided, Catherine. I didn't know how your little commune was playing out in that town. I knew the townspeople would love to gossip about you, and I took advantage of it. For all we know, so did his attorneys."

Catherine felt deflated, like a balloon that had been popped.

Dr. Lindberg and Jenny entered the room with plates of sandwiches and bottles of soda.

"Chicken or roast beef?" Farley asked.

By the time Daniel and his lawyers returned, the afternoon depositions started closer to 2:30 than 2:00 p.m. Catherine wondered how much longer her attorney would take and tried to pay closer attention to the questions. She avoided watching Daniel. It pained her to glance at him sitting at the end of the table as he showed no emotion on his face. Daniel was being peppered with questions so simple his attorney's couldn't find a reason to not allow them. She began to wonder if her attorney was really doing this properly. By the smirks on Daniel's attorneys' faces, the way they sat comfortably leaning back in their seats, and their reassuring nods to Daniel, Catherine thought maybe it was going too well for *them.*

"With regard to the mental health evaluation, gentlemen," Farley continued.

Everyone sat up straighter, including Catherine.

"Dr. Lindberg has done some extensive testing that was just finished yesterday, and I have copies for your files."

Jenny handed out the copies from a stack in front of her. The attorneys began to scan the pages immediately with their eyes.

Farley began, "Here's the thing. Catherine's previous doctor has come out in defense of you, Mr. Janson. First of all, he was *her* doctor. He betrayed her confidences in an effort to make her behave the way he thinks a wife should— really none of his business."

"Secondly, Mr. Janson has no proof that the farm was unfit for the children, or that Catherine's friends moving in were detrimental to their well-being. I interviewed the children's teachers myself. Here is a copy of those interviews." He nodded toward Jenny, who passed out the next pile of pages.

"And, as to having the divorce tried in Massachusetts, there's one detail that makes that out of the question. Jenny?"

Jenny produced one sheet of paper—a copy of the town's records.

"Technically, both Mr. and Mrs. Janson are legal residents of Vermont.

The silence was deafening.

Daniel's entire group of attorney's turned toward him. His head tilted down as he looked in disbelief at the copy of the town's voting registration which made Vermont their legal residence. *The Town Meeting when property owners were asked to sign.*

"I forgot," he said, eyes lowered as he read the document.

Catherine knew what it meant—her divorce had to go through the courts of Vermont, not Massachusetts, and that meant the threat of being institutionalized and losing her children was less—possibly non-existent.

Tears of relief flowed down her cheeks.

...Our house is a very very, very fine house
With two cats in the yard
Life used to be so hard
Now everything is easy
'Cause of you...

Graham Nash, Crosby, Stills, Nash & Young,
"Our House," *Déjà Vu,* 1970

Chapter 19

Now that she had lived through the depositions, and the custody of her daughters at least for the school year was secured, Catherine felt ready to move on—and create— a new life.

Since Christmas vacation would arrive soon enough and the girls would go to their father's, Cat tried to visit Sam and Cheryl during the week for supper, and Saturdays, until she had to drive them to Boston.

The Wednesday evening before, Cheryl said she would bring up the idea of them all living together. Perhaps coming from her, it would seem like a fun idea.

"That would be great, Cheryl. Just one thing, before we move in, you have to get a telephone. The girls have to be able to call their dad."

Cheryl laughed. "Probably about time!"

Cat thought she handled all of it very well, but Sam wasn't that keen about having a phone.

As they sat around the table, drinking mint tea and eating carob brownies[19], Cheryl turned to the girls.

"Well, Laura, Becky, we have a very big house here and lots of things to do because we have so many pets to take care of. When it's time to leave the farmhouse, do you think you and your mother would like to move in with Sam and me and help us with the dog and the kittens?"

"Oh, yes!" Laura said.

"I can help," said Becky.

"Girls, if it's really all right with you both, when you return from Boston, we could be all moved in here," Cat said.

"Yippee! Yippee!" Laura and Becky jumped up and down and hugged their mother first, and then they hugged Cheryl and Sam.

After taking the girls to Boston, Cat returned to spend the last night in the farmhouse. The next morning, Cheryl and Sam arrived bright and early to help load up the pieces of furniture that she was keeping, her clothing and her books. They walked through the barn to check for any of Cheryl and Sam's items left from moving the tepee. One carved peg for tethering the perimeter of the tepee to the ground was left by itself on a work bench. Sam picked it up. Cat paused at the window that looked down into the front parlor, thinking of that night when she and Sam were in the barn.

Over the few weeks since Thanksgiving, Cat had packed her desk, her clothes and shoes, and her sewing and knitting baskets. It wasn't as bad as she thought it would be. Packing up the girls' things wasn't too bad, either. They had toy boxes that contained all their toys, blocks, dolls and games. And, their books were mixed in with Cat's books so they were all packed and boxed together.

It took the rest of the day to clear everything out and move it to Cheryl and Sam's home. Cat went back that night to clean. She had decided then that she would sleep one more night at the farmhouse—she needed to. She called Cheryl to let her know.

The next morning, Sam showed up by himself. When Cat went to the door, they embraced and hugged and kissed like they would never see each other again. They went into the front room. The furniture she was keeping was already moved and the few rugs were gone as well. All

Cat had left was her sleeping bag. They unzipped it and spread it out on the floor.

After they pleased each other for what seemed like a long time, Sam said, "We need to leave, Catherine." He had used her full name. She didn't like it because it reminded her of Daniel when he was angry with her.

"Just call me, Cat. Okay?"

"Sure."

He stood up to dress and she traced his back and legs with her eyes, wondering if there would be any more intimate time when she moved in with Sam and Cheryl. *How will I feel watching them together?*

"I need to walk through the house first," Cat said, buttoning up her flannel shirt and pulling on her jeans.

"Sure," said Sam.

Cat went to the barn through the family room, climbed to the third floor and looked around the space, empty except for some old sleighs and rusted relics of early farm life. She looked at the beams and the color of the wood, and marveled that the house and barn had stood there for such a long time. Then, she looked at the second floor where she and Sam had made love Thanksgiving evening.

The long, empty workbench was worn round and smooth from years of use—not to mention the excitement over Thanksgiving when it still held Scott's marijuana plants.

Then, she went down the stairs and into the family room that was cold and empty, she climbed the ladder to the loft, an open space that held many memories, and back down to the hallway into the kitchen. She closed the door from the cold.

She knew the owners would be moving in within a day or two so she set the heat to keep the pipes from freezing, and turned on the kitchen and bathroom faucets. She had told them she would leave the phone on as it could take a week or two to get one. "It's too far from town not to have a phone," she had said, thinking of all of her experiences when she was there alone. It would be different now with a "normal" family living there. No one in town would bother them.

There were certain artifacts she left that came with the farm; oxen pulls, wagon wheels, old tools, things that belonged there. But, not the shotgun that had hung over the mantel. That would stay with her.

Sam was in the front room and had rolled up her sleeping bag and stuffed it in its sack. "Ready, Cat?" he asked.

"Ready, Sam, let's go."

...All these places had their moments
With lovers and friends I still can recall
Some are dead and some are living
In my life I've loved them all...

John Lennon and Paul McCartney,

"In My Life," The Beatles, *Rubber Soul*, 1965

I want to thank some of those who participated in the commune as friends, lovers and others, and brought some love, some time, for some reason. In my life, I loved them all.

Alan and Witchy, Barbara and Bob, Barbara and Myles, Cathy and Mark, Celeste, Click, Dee and Johnny, Gail and Hen, Gail and Joe, Gina and Dale, Heather and Tom, Janet and Jay, Jeannie and Larry, Jeff, Judy, Kenny, Leah and Harry, Marcia, Nancy and Frank, Pam and Stephen, Paul, Ronnie, Scott, Shawn and Guy, Steven, Susie and Zunk, Tommy, and, of course,

The Kentucky brothers...

...But you got to have friends.
The feelings oh so strong.
You got to have friends
To make that day last long...

Bette Midler, Songwriters: Klingman, Mark; Buzzy Linhart, "Friends," *The Divine Miss M,* 1972

In Gratitude

To Tracy, Blake, Tammy, Marco, Hinmaton, Samantha, Pram Dass and Nicole, you are the best people in my life, my reason to become better than I used to be. None of my writing would have been possible without you in my life. Thank you.

And to the lights of my spirit who remind me to play: Dante, Nicholas, Tyler, Aodhan and Hudson.

To Barbara Tierney for taking me in during my days of slender means, and providing a haven from the storm.

To Beth Redstone from Taos. I hope we meet again.

To Diana Webber, thank you for your continued reassurance that I could complete one novel at a time, for weekends in Rockport and your belief in me. You are my favorite sister!

To Janet and Jay Booker who give me writing weekends in their country setting, feed my body and soul, show up when I am in need, and love me unconditionally. You are my angels.

To Naomi Lake, who believes that I can do it, casts light into darkness, and supported me at my very first writer's award in Albuquerque. Your friendship is an underlying current that travels with me.

To Peggy Atwood, who talks me into not giving up, sent me to swim with wild dolphins, and never forgets who I am even when I do. Your consistent commitment to our friendship makes all the difference.

To Sue and Frank Anthony, New England Writers, who taught me to keep submitting until I won. You may have crossed over, but your encouragement and influence will live on for many, many poets and writers.

Long may you run.

A Vegetarian In A Fox Fur Coat

In 2010, publication of the second novel in the trilogy, *A Vegetarian In A Fox Fur Coat,* continues the journey from the commune in Vermont to building an intentional community in the middle of 55 acres of land in New Hampshire.

As Cat, Cheryl and Sam dream of self-sufficiency, the return of Cat's friends from the commune is cause for celebration and new hopes, however, not all will turn out as planned. Living in tepees while building cabins in the woods begins easily enough. But, the mercurial New England weather, and the shifting relationships, creates hardships inside the fragile community that threatens to split it apart. Going back to the land with small children, animals, and two pregnant women, twenty miles from nowhere, seemed like a good idea at the time...

You may order Once Upon A Commune at:

http://abilenegray.com

[1] **Ram Dass** first went to India in 1967. He was still Dr. Richard Alpert, an already eminent Harvard psychologist and psychedelic pioneer with Dr. Timothy Leary. He had continued his psychedelic research until that fateful Eastern trip in 1967, when he traveled to India. In India, he met his guru, Neem Karoli Baba, affectionately known as Maharajji, who gave Ram Dass his name, which means "servant of God." Everything changed then - his intense dharmic life started, and he became a pivotal influence on a culture that has reverberated with the words "Be Here Now" ever since. Ram Dass's spirit has been a guiding light for three generations, carrying along millions on the journey, helping free them from their bonds as he has worked his way through his own.

Since 1968, Ram Dass has pursued a panoramic array of spiritual methods and practices from potent ancient wisdom traditions, including bhakti or devotional yoga focused on the Hindu deity Hanuman; Buddhist meditation in the Theravadin, Mahayana Tibetan and Zen Buddhist schools, and Sufi and Jewish mystical studies. Perhaps most significantly, his practice of karma yoga or spiritual service has opened up millions of other souls to their deep, yet individuated spiritual practice and path. Ram Dass continues to uphold the bodhisattva ideal for others through his compassionate sharing of true knowledge and vision. His unique skill in getting people to cut through and feel divine love without dogma is still a positive influence on many, many people from all over the planet.

Ram Dass biography quoted from:
(http://www.ramdass.org/Biography/tabid/331/Default.aspx)

[2] **Jere Bishop Franco**, *Crossing the Pond: The Native American Effort in World War II, 1999.*

While the phrase is often accredited to the British idiom, quote:

"Crossing the Pond" is a term Native Americans used to describe the process of being transferred overseas for military duty. This was both an event and a duty taken quite seriously by tribal members, who participated in every aspect of war-time America....

[3] **Ian Bradley** (1996). *The Complete Annotated Gilbert & Sullivan.* Oxford: Oxford University Press.

Green Grow The Rushes, Ho (or *O*) (aka *The Twelve Prophets,* or *The Carol Of The Twelve Numbers,* or *The Teaching Song,* or *The Dilly Song*), is a folk song (Roud #133) popular across the English speaking world. It is sometimes sung as a Christmas carol...It is cumulative in structure, with each verse built up from the previous verse by appending a new stanza...

Quoted from:(http://www.hymnsandcarolsofchristmas.com)

[4] **Deborah Markowitz**, Vermont Secretary of State, "A Citizen's Guide To Vermont Town Meeting" ..."On Town Meeting Day, the first Tuesday in March, citizens across Vermont come together in their communities to discuss the business of their towns. For over 200 years Town Meeting Day has been an important political event as Vermonters elect local officers and vote on budgets. It has also

been a time for neighbors to discuss the civic issues of their community, state, and nation."

Quoted from: A Vermont Government Website, Copyright© 2004 State of Vermont All rights reserved(http://www.sec.state.vt.us/TownMeeting/citizens_guide.html)

[5] **Afro** [af-roh]
    -*adjective*
    1. of or pertaining to Afro-Americans or to black traditions, culture, etc.:
        Afro societies; Afro hair styles.
    -noun
    2.a hair style originating with black persons, in which the hair is
        allowed to grow naturally and to acquire a bushy appearance.
    Origin:
    1965-1970; independent use of AFRO
    Quoted from: (http://dictionary.reference.com)

[6]**Tom Jones,** a well-known 60's pop singer from Wales, was also know for wearing an Edwardian- style shirt that became very cool to wear during the 60's and 70's. McCall's created a pattern named "Tom Jones Shirt/Blouse and Flared Skirt Pattern McCalls 7378" which was all the rage.

    Quoted from a listing that may no longer link: (<u>1960s *Tom Jones Shirt*</u>/<u>Blouse and Flared Skirt pattern McCalls 7378 ...</u>Mar 18, 2009 ... Vintage 60's McCall's "printed" pattern for a "*Tom* Joes *Shirt*" Blouse and Flared Skirt with optional patch pockets. Dated 1964.)
        (...www.etsy.com/view_listing.php?listing_id=6911649)

[7] **Robert A. Brooks, JD, PhD**, author of *Psychiatrists' Opinions About Involuntary Civil Commitment: Results of a National Survey.* Copyright©2007 by the American Academy of Psychiatry and the Law.
"Involuntary civil commitment laws provide for the forceful detention and commitment to an institution by judicial means of persons with mental illnesses who meet certain further criteria. These particular criteria vary from state to state and have also been subject to historical trends. Until the late 1960s many states, operating under their *parens patriae* powers, allowed for the commitment of persons who had a mental illness and simply needed treatment...."

    Quoted from: (http://www.jaapl.org/cgi/content/abstract/35/2/219)

[8] **The *Real Paper*,** a Massachusetts alternative weekly, was descended from the *Cambridge Phoenix*, which began publishing in the fall of 1969. The '60s counterculture was building to high tide, and it was an auspicious time to launch an underground journal.

The decade's alternative press in the Boston area got its start much earlier, apparently with David Wilson's newsletter, *The Broadside*, in December 1962. Its purpose was quite straightforward--to let Boston folk music fans know about upcoming shows. The Boston-Cambridge coffeehouse community, just like today, was quite strong. And though the musicians and fans were not necessarily very political, nonetheless it makes sense that the area's counterculture should begin with its folkies--they were numerous, their music was a clear alternative to the commercial-radio/major-label mainstream, and a few of the artists were known to draw '60s-style inspiration from certain chemicals of questionable legality...

Quoted from: *The Real Paper*(http://www.geocities.com/uridfm/r/realpaper.htm)
(Author still has the section of The Real Paper with the referred-to-photograph.)

[9] **The Orson Welles Cinema**, 1001 Massachusetts Avenue, Cambridge, MA 02138 ran a film school during the 70's.

The Orson Welles Cinema began life in the early 1960's as the Esquire Theatre. Later the name was changed to the Orson Welles Cinema. Over the years two small additional screening rooms were added that were separate from the larger main auditorium...The theatre specialized in first run art and independent films, and had some occasional revival series. In the mid-1980s there was a fire in the theatre, and it was shuttered after that and the space put to other commercial use...
Quoted from: (http://cinematreasures.org/theater/6492/)

[10] **Chakras** –so many books about chakras are available to understand the body's energy systems but this website should not be missed.

(http://jksalescompany.com/dw/chakra.html)

[11] **Gopi Krishna**, Kundalini-*The Evolutionary Energy in Man,* Shambala, 1971.

Krishna's writings influenced Western readers with his explanations of the unconscious force of the goddess Shakti sleeping at the base of the spine like a serpent.

The website: (http://www.webonautics.com/mythology/shakti.html) gives a great deal of information describing Shakti's importance in Hinduism.

[12] Song or chant written by **Paramhansa Yogananda** and said "Thee" in place of "you." Paramhansa Yogananda (1893-1952, often misspelled "Paramahansa" Yogananda) was the first yoga master of India to take up permanent residence in the West. Yogananda arrived in America in 1920, and traveled throughout the United States on what he called his "spiritual campaigns." His enthusiastic audiences filled the largest halls in America. Hundreds of thousands came to see the yogi from India. Yogananda continued to lecture and write up to his passing in 1952...

Yogananda's initial impact was truly impressive. But his lasting impact has been even greater. Yogananda's *Autobiography of a Yogi*, first published in 1946, helped launch a spiritual revolution in the West. His message was nonsectarian and universal. Yogananda's teacher sent him to the West with the admonition, "The West is high in material attainments, but lacking in spiritual understanding. It is God's will that you play a role in teaching mankind the value of balancing the material with an inner, spiritual life."

Biographical information quoted from:
(http://www.ananda.org/ananda/yogananda.html)

[13] **Gloria Steinem** was the founding editor and publisher of *Ms. Magazine* in 1972 as well as a prominent political leader in the women's rights movement of the 1960s and 1970s.

Paraphrased from: (http://en.wikipedia.org/wiki/Gloria_Steinem)

[14] **The A.I.M. Song**

"Origins: The origins of the song itself are uncertain, and there are various theories attributing the song to various locations across North America and various points in history. For many tribes, the origins of the song have been legendized.

A popular theory is that it developed from a simple song hummed by a child at Crow Fair. This is possible, because the vocables are not particularly complex, however the claim remains largely ungrounded.

A more likely theory is that it was developed between two early members of the American Indian Movement. Edward Benton-Banai, from the Lac Courte Oreilles Band of Ojibwe Indians, co-founded the movement in 1972, and is rumoured as the songwriter. The song could have been inspired by a traditional Ojibwe honoring song, known as the Air force Song.

Severt Young Bear, an Oglala Lakota from Porcupine, South Dakota, was also involved in AIM. As the lead singer of the Porcupine Singers, he made the song popular in the early 1970s. Although he admits he did not write it, collaboration between himself and Benton-Banai could have helped the song to develop."

Quoted from: (http://en.wikipedia.org/wiki/AIM Song)

[15] **Jen Miller**, "Frybread," *Smithsonian* magazine, July 2008

"...Navajo frybread originated 144 years ago, when the United States forced Indians living in Arizona to make the 300-mile journey known as the "Long Walk" and relocate to New Mexico, onto land that couldn't easily support their traditional staples of vegetables and beans. To prevent the indigenous populations from starving, the government gave them canned goods as well as white flour, processed sugar and lard—the makings of frybread.

Frybread appears to be nothing more than fried dough—like an unsweetened funnel cake, but thicker and softer, full of air bubbles and reservoirs of grease—but it is revered by some as a symbol of Native pride and unity. Indian rocker Keith Secola celebrates the food in his popular song "Frybread." In Sherman Alexie's award-winning film *Smoke Signals*, one character wears a "Frybread Power" T-shirt. Both men call frybread today's most relevant Native American symbol. They say the food's conflicted status—it represents both perseverance and pain—reflects these same elements in Native American history...."

Quoted from (http://www.smithsonianmag.com/people-places/frybread.html)

[16] **The American Indian Movement** history and archives websites:

(http://www.aimovement.org/ggc/history.html)
(http://www.aimovement.org/archives/index.html)

[17] **Giveaway,** Native American religious practices...Generosity in the Native American tradition, is a religious act as well as a social one. The value of generosity is perhaps most dramatically figured in the northern practice known in English as giveaway or in the potlatch of the Northwest Coast peoples, in which property and gifts are ceremonially distributed...

Quoted from:(http://www.britannica.com/EBchecked/topic/1080979/giveaway)

[18] **Ray Richard**, *The Boston Sunday Globe*—October 23, 1966. "Can Freedom Be a Whim of Justice?"

...Frank Anthony (Abilene Gray's paraphrasing) took up an interest in releasing a person who was later found to be unjustly institutionalized after Dr. Thomas Szasz published *Psychiatric Justice*. Dr. Szasz wrote that once anyone is committed to a mental hospital the burden of proving competency rests with him, not with his examiners...

When I was in the Anthony's living room in Vermont, Frank gave me a photocopy of this article in a discussion regarding the way in which institutionalization laws could be interpreted depending upon the medical professions' views at the time.

[19] **Jason Horn**, "The 70's Revisited," Published March 14, 2007

"Q: Is carob really healthier than chocolate?

A: When your hippie mother fed it to you in the '70s, she thought carob was a miracle replacement for chocolate. And it is ever so slightly healthier in a few respects. Unlike cocoa, carob does not contain caffeine or theobromine, another mild stimulant that actually elevates mood in humans but is the reason large quantities of chocolate are dangerous to dogs and cats. (They metabolize the chemical more slowly than we do, so it can build up in their bodies, poisoning them). People who are allergic to chocolate can generally eat carob without a problem (as can dogs and cats)..."

Quoted from: (http://www.chow.com/stories/10491)

Author's Note: These Notes and quotes are meant to illuminate the times and offer ideas for further research if interested.